Dragon's Prize is a work of fiction. All names, characters, places and incidents are the product of the author's imagination or used fictitiously and any resemblance to any actual persons, living or dead, events or locales is entirely coincidental. This is the property and ownership of the author and any reproduction, electronic or otherwise, without the express permission of the author without copy write permission will be prosecuted to the fullest extent of the law.

Reviews: 5 Stars
"Romantic, suspenseful, fantasy/sci-fi."

"Excellent! The author keeps you intrigued and engaged!"

I0520394

Acknowledgements

Ebook Launch: Dane/Jon/Adrian at
http://ebooklaunch.com
Beta Readers: Patricia Walsh, Melissa, and Aleacia
Webmaster: RD for www.bjbrandon.com

Other acknowledgements:
General Motors Company, Denali
Pave Military Helicopter

This one is also for Retha and Wayne Barton, who took a girl in when she needed a place to land and taught her how to look at the world differently.

"Believe you can . . . and you're halfway there!"

For all those who believe all is lost and there is no hope, look up and see the sunshine. If there is no sunshine, find one thing to make you smile. Pay it forward and it will lift you up and it will be worth the effort. The saying "what goes around comes around" is so true, so pay a smile or a helping hand forward. You may need it again someday.

Table of Contents

Prologue

A long forgotten prophecy foretold of a young babe born of royal blood carrying unique gifts only the Learned could possess. Laydya Valeyrian's lonely path destiny is fraught with dangers so evil and so dark that few would venture to help except for Dougal, the Captain of the Guards. After the death of her father, he has taught a lonely Laydya how to survive. Lowen the Priestess of the Order, tried to become the mother she never knew and guide her once her gifts finally manifest into the powerful tools she would need if she were to survive their journey. When Valeyrian Keep is almost decimated by Kasadim's dark forces the three of them flee with only Damen, Laydya's childhood pet, an orphaned panther she hand raised. Their only chance is for Lowen to finally impart the ways of the Learned to her young charge in order for Laydya to survive and hopefully vanquish Kasadim. Otherwise, it is not just the lands of Valeyrian that will fall, but all of the surrounding kingdoms.

Gavilan's acceptance of both Laydya's gifts and the quest she must follow test both of them along the way until they reach the Circle of Stones where Lowen is determined to transfer the ancient knowledge to Laydya necessary to complete her mission. The devil hounds chasing them to the Circle of Stones nearly take out Dougal, but Lowen must first concentrate on Laydya.

Lowen can't forewarn the others of what will take place once they reach the Stones or what she must due to heal Dougal once she has transferred all she can to her young charge. All she can do is trust that the Fates' have chosen wisely.

The prophecy is alive.

Chapter 1

It was the sound of sobbing that awoke him. A deep, gut-wrenching sound that cut into Gavilan's soul and pulled at something he thought long dead. He knew that he hadn't heard such grief or despair since the last engagement he and his men had taken against the accursed devils they couldn't kill, and it scared his very soul to hear it again. Gavilan sat up, bringing his dagger from inside his tall boot as he came up against the tree at his back.   The Laydya sat huddled as she curled around the black back her pet sobbing uncontrollably.   Her hands curled into Damen's neck while the panther licked tears from her face but Laydya seemed not to notice.   One look at her, and Gavilan's sense of foreboding returned with a vengeance.   Before Gavilan could get up to go to her, Dougal groaned from across the way, holding his side.

Gavilan turned to him, could see the shivers wracking his body as fever continued to ravage the elder warrior from the wound festering in his side.   Lowen sat next to him, a cloth on his forehead, her other hand lovingly patting Dougal's chest.   Gavilan met Lowen's tired eyes and cringed at what he saw there.

Death, sorrow, and a pain so deep it made his chest ache.

"Is there nothing you can do?" he asked the Druidess, moving as close as he dared.

"I was about to do so, but I need to talk to you first." She dipped the cloth in the bowl next to her and put the cloth back onto Dougal's forehead, turning back to Gavilan. "My strength is drained, and what will happen in the next few minutes you cannot stop.   Dougal gave me his promise. However, I must have yours as well.   Swear to me, on the blood of your ancestors that you will get the two of them to

Dragonslair as soon as possible. It is the only salvation any of you have to survive!"

"How did you know . . .?"

"Stop being thickheaded boy, because it matters not right now!" she swore, swiping her hands in the air. "Listen to me, Gavilan. I must have your promise. There isn't much time!"

She drilled him with her gaze, willing him to accept her words on face value. It was something that was hard for Gavilan to do with anything or anyone, especially those who dealt with magic of any kind. He watched the old woman's tired smile lighten her face a bit and it almost made him feel like a small boy caught in the pantry again.

"I realize you don't trust easily, but remember your brother. His gifts are not evil. Not all magic is what it seems, and many are gifts to be treasured and protected. A precious gift that can save our lands and keep all safe if you will follow your heart instead that stubborn head of yours. Sometimes . . ." she paused, looking wistfully down at the man she tended, "Sometimes we have to trust our hearts to lead us. Now you must make your choice. I must have your promise, of your own free will."

"Are you saying you could force me if you wished?" he asked, astounded.

"Aye, but I will not," was all Lowen countered.

Gavilan studied her a minute, seeing the fatigue and something else just under the surface. Lowen looked more fragile in the pre-dawn light, almost breakable somehow. He couldn't put his finger on it, but he sensed something was very wrong with her, and he was positive he wasn't going to like it one bit!

"Alright, witch. You have my vow upon the honor of my spurs as a knight and a leader of men. If I can save us, I will give my life to do so." He heard her soft sigh, watched her shoulders wilt before his eyes. He made a move toward her but Lowen held up her hand to stop him from he could even touch her. She pushed herself up on tired legs and stood tall.

"Do not try to touch me again, young man. And make sure this old fool does not try, either." She smiled a tired smile, and removed a pouch from a deep pocket in her robe. Opening it, she poured out a stone, blood red in color, and emitting a pulsing light from its core. She bent down and placed the stone in the center of Dougal's chest. With a sigh, Lowen closed her eyes and extended her arms out from her body with hands flat, she raised them to the heavens. Her long, slender fingers hovered inches above Dougal's chest, all the while drawing energy from everything around her.

"With this stone I leach out the poison of evil which has been sent by one from afar, and entrust the soul of this man to the gods that protect all of us. From me, to thee, I give you life." A soft radiance sprinkled down from her hands, and entered the stone.

Standing there, Gavilan couldn't believe his eyes. The stone seem to come alive even if such a thing were possible. It began to pulse, and rays of fiery red reached out across Dougal and sank into his heated skin. The old warrior moaned once, then jerked as if having a bad dream, then lay still. A long silence held everyone in the small area in its grasps as if nature waited, but Gavilan couldn't have guessed what it was it waited for. He was stunned when Dougal opened his eyes with a bewildered expression on his face, like waking from a long, dreamless sleep.

"Nooooo . . ." The scream came from Laydya's direction, and Gavilan turned to watch her wobble up from her pallet with tears pouring down her face. "You can't do this, Lowen. Don't leave me, please!" she screamed, stumbling toward the Druidess.

"Gavilan, hold her . . . please!" Lowen whispered, then took several steps back from all of them.

"What the hell is happening?" Gavilan yelled as he grabbed Laydya when she lurched toward the older woman, penning Laydya within the circle of his massive arms. Laydya fought him, kicking and screaming as she tried everything in her power to escape his tight grasp. Finally, she slumped to the ground, her sobs tearing at his soul.

Dougal was now awake, but didn't seem to understand what was happening until Lowen caught his eyes with hers. One look at the Druidess, and his warrior's battle cry echoed off the walls of the Circle of Stones in anguish even though he couldn't have moved if his life depended on it. The stone on his chest weighted him down as Lowen had meant it to, effectively keeping him from being able to touch her.

Gavilan looked at the girl sobbing on the ground, at the old warrior beating his fist against the packed earth and listened as the huge cat's continued screams echoing into the early dawn, a mirror of the torment to what his mistress was feeling. Finally. his eyes found the Druidess, and comprehension almost brought him to his knees.
An iridescent web of almost invisible threads began to form out of thin air, slowly working their way in a gossamer web around the Druidess, weaving a cocoon so gentle yet solid as it swayed back and forth. The webbing continued as the gilded cage surrounded the Druidess from head to toe. Gavilan started toward her, intent on trying to help no matter his earlier promise but was stopped by her words.

"No, Gavilan, you must not come near. I have expended my energies to their limit, and must now pay the price. Only by completing her quest, can Laydya set me free," came a wispy voice out of the thickening mass of glittering threads.

"Dougal, listen to me, for there is not much time. This is not forever, my love.   You must believe that." Dougal's strangled grunt was the only acknowledgment the warrior could manage, for he had finally realized that she had just given her life for the two people she loved most in this world.   Never for a moment did he believe that she could come back to him.   First and foremost, he was a warrior, and knew the costs associated with war . . . and this evil that pursued them would end in war.

"Gavilan, remember your promise.   Do not forsake it . . . you destiny and Laydya's depend on it.   Trust you heart!"   Gavilan heard the words in his mind rather than his ears, and he shook his head trying to clear it.   He gazed at the almost solid wall of softly glowing gossamer fibers, and blanched. He could still see Lowen's small form inside, but her mouth was curved in a gentle smile, her eyes closed.

Laydya finally rose and stood on her own legs, swaying back and forth.

"Yes," she mumbled softly.   "I hear you.   I will do as you ask, but I don't have to like it."   There was an audible chuckle on the wind, causing the flesh to rise on Gavilan's neck.   She cocked her head slightly, as if listening, then looked at Gavilan with a shocked expression.   When she looked back at the cocoon, Laydya could only shake her head.

"Why didn't you tell me?" she shouted, then paled.   "I see.   I promise, on the grave of my father, and on the Valeyrian Lands I hold in trust, I will succeed, or die trying!"

Suddenly, all was quiet within the Circle of Stones. Damen lay next to the cocoon, watching his mistress with eyes so like hers.   Dougal lay back against the stone wall, tears flowing unchecked down his bearded face.

And Gavilan . . .

He prayed that the Gods would be merciful, because he

intended to make whoever was responsible for all of the death and destruction that had stalked them so far pay.

Pay with their lives!

Chapter 2

"How can I go with you, when you don't even believe in what we are doing? You think only a sword and brute strength can win the day!" Laydya yelled at the stone-faced warrior standing not even an arm's length from her. They had been arguing since dawn, neither of them willing to give an inch, both determined their method was the right one.

"Lowen gave her life for us! You witnessed her transformation, yet you still don't believe. What will it take, a dragon tearing your black heart out and shoving it in your face to make you believe all of this?" She pushed past him, determined to finish packing and get away from the Circle. Every time she looked at the cocoon where the Druidess was encased, her heart nearly broke all over again. She wasn't prepared for a rough hand grasping her arm.

"I gave my word as a warrior and a knight. We go to Dragonslair, and that's final. From there, we can make plans for what will come. We cannot take Dougal any farther than that, or he'll die, and Lowen would have given the last of her strength for aught?" His voice was low but stern, and Laydya was surprised to finally see the knight who had led such brave men against all odds. Looking into his deep green eyes, she knew this was one fight she wasn't going to win, no matter how hard she fought.

"How many days' ride is it to your home?" she finally asked, her ire quickly replaced by a hot heat that spread from where his hand held her arm, coursing throughout her entire body. The question sounded lame to her ears, but at the mention of Dragonslair, Gavilan's eyes brightened.

"We can be there in two days' time. The passage that will allow us to cross the mountains isn't far, if Dougal's memory is sound." He turned away, but was brought up short by Damen sitting directly behind him. In fact, he almost tripped over the cat, the animal was so close.

Gavilan looked from the cat to Laydya, then knelt down in front of the black feline so that his eyes were almost even with the golden ones staring at him. He took the cat's massive head in both hands and rubbed his ears, whispering low so Laydya couldn't make out the words. Then, the huge warrior stood and walked away, leaving her to stare after him dumbfounded.

She watched him walk away, then knelt next to Damen.

"Traitor," she whispered, rubbing his ears. Watching Gavilan's muscles move under his tight shirt as he packed their belongings in anticipation of their journey, she marveled at the change that had come over him. It was as if he were driven by some unseen force to protect all of them. Of course, she told herself, it could just be his male stubbornness coming to the surface after being dormant for so long. But Laydya didn't think so. She could sense a profound change in him . . . one that made a small flame of hope begin to burn brightly in her. Maybe, just maybe, he would finally accept that not everyone who had a `gift' was evil.

With a sigh, Laydya shoved back terrifying thoughts of "what if" and rose to help break camp. The trip would be hardest on Dougal since his fever had just broken and his body was weak. She still wasn't exactly sure what Lowen had done while using the bloodstone, but Laydya knew some of its properties. Among others, it was used by the Learned and Healers to pull poisons from patients, clean the blood from impurities, and lend health the one who wore it. A Blessed Bloodstone was imbedded in the hilt of Laydya's own sword, a gift from her grandfather when Dougal had commissioned the sword to be made to fit her hands. Lowen had told her the stone bestowed the worthy person who carried sword courage and strength. She could only pray the Druidess was right because she was determined to keep Dougal safe and out of as much pain as possible now that she was responsible for all of them.

She went through their belongs, making sure she had Lowen's herbal bag close at hand. With a sigh that sounded like it bore the weight of all of the kingdoms, Laydya removed the bloodstone from Dougal's dozing for, tucking it into a hidden pocket of her tunic. If worse came to worse, she would use it again, but Lowen had cautioned her to be careful with it. Its power could alert Kasadim of their location, and she was to avoid that at all costs.

Looking at the silvery cocoon that held the only mother she had ever known, Laydya felt tears threaten to spill but she forced them back. Gavilan and Dougal couldn't know to what extent Lowen's sacrifice had been, but she did. The force of the cocoon would keep unseen eyes focused on the Circle of Stones for a long while, allowing the small party to make their way safely over the pass and out of Kasadim's reach.

At least for a while! Her sacrifice would allow them to escape, but it would be up to Laydya to make sure the Druidess didn't die. As long as the essence of Lowen flowed within her pupil, she would live. If Laydya failed, they would all die!

Chapter 3

Dragonslair Keep

Eric knew he was in big trouble!

After dispatching the messengers as he had promised, after adding a little more information to the one to Laydya's grandfather, Eric had sought out his father.   He now stood before him in the great hall as the tall, imposing ruler of one of the largest kingdoms in the country, ranted at what Lord Invor considered clear stupidity by his youngest son and designated heir.

"Do you realize the danger you put yourself in, *you*, the heir to *this* keep, by your irresponsible actions?"   Lord Invor didn't expect an answer, nor did he wait for one. "All for that good-for-nothing brother of yours!   You went chasing after him, because of some dream!"   His father paced in front of a huge chair that sat on a platform overlooking the hall.

"I exiled Gavilan for his own good, you know, and for yours!   Now you tell me you have been studying with these . . . Druids, the same ones I banished years ago for unspeakable crimes!"   Lord Invor was furious, yep, there was no doubt about it.   He was turning a mottled red from the rage he was trying so hard to control.

"Eric, if you are going to rule in this chair someday, you have to learn some common sense.   How in the name of all that is holy do I teach it to you?"

His sire ran a shaky hand through long grey hair, spreading the thick mane down the back of his robes like some avenging angel's silken hair.

"It is not my throne, Sire, and well you know it!"   Eric said softly, but he might as well have shouted it to the whole Keep.   Lord Invor's advisors gasped at Eric's open defiance, and the serving women scattered like frightened mice as they exited the room through every available doorway.

"Do not bring it up again, Eric! We are not going to discuss it, and that is final!" Lord Invor shouted as he stood toe to toe with his youngest son. Eric realized he had probably pushed his father to his limit, at least for the moment. He dared not say another word, but he saw the naked truth in his sire's eyes.

The pain of banishing Gavilan was slowly eating away his father's soul. Gavilan was the oldest and once favorite son! His father's anger was known far and wide, and now pride forbade Lord of Dragonslair from calling his son back home.

Gavilan's mother had died giving birth, and Invor had always cherished the boy with green eyes and an adventuresome nature so like his mother's, but when the boy turned five summers, all of that changed! The woman who had attended his young wife during childbirth came forward with a hideous secret she felt needed to be aired claiming she could not hide it any longer. Invor had believed the midwife/healer when she told him tales of his young innocent wife's supposed liaisons with Invor's closest friend, trying to discredit her in his eyes. The midwife claimed to have seen his lovely wife in several passionate trysts with the wizard from Dragonslair court, a crime punishable by death!

Lord Invor hadn't been able to bear even the slightest possibility that Gavilan wasn't his true son. Unable to stand the sight of the boy, he sent him to be fostered at another large holding on the other side of the mountains, removing any possibility that he would see the small boy. Then he took another wife, determined to sire another heir who would be true to Dragonslair, untainted by scandal and magic!

Eric was born, as well as two daughters, and Invor

disinherited Gavilan, claiming Eric as heir.   It came as a shock to the entire land when the healer had been struck down with a wasting disease, and had begged her overlord to come to her deathbed.

There she finally admitted to her lies against the young mistress she had envied before her death.   Some of it was caused by jealousy, while the rest was from superstition for the young beauty from an unknown and faraway place. Believing that in telling the truth, her sickness would be cured, the old woman had told everything, including the names of the noblemen in Invor's own castle who had plotted with her to overthrow Dragonslair!   She died two days later, in greater agony than any person in Dragonslair had ever seen.   However, the damage couldn't be undone. Gavilan had been disinherited long ago and Eric was his heir by law and in the eyes of the people.

"Father . . ."   Eric placed his hand on his parent's shoulder.   He could feel the turmoil in his Sire, but there was no way he could explain how he knew.   Instead, Eric offered what little comfort he could.

"Let us not rehash this, not when more pressing matters demand our attention.   Gavilan is safe, for now.   We have to get ready.   It isn't a matter of *if* there will be a battle, but *when..*"

A nod was his father's only response.   Lord Invor retreated to studying the strategies spread on a large table near the wall.   With defenses of their holdings fortified as much as possible and watches placed so ample warning could be given if mischief came to light, they could only wait.

Eric's father was a brilliant warrior who had seen many battles in his younger years, but waiting was not in Eric's nature.   He needed to know what was going on, and that Gavilan was really safe.   The only way to find that out was to use the knowledge taught to him by the Order.

Collecting the necessary items he would need, Eric sought out a special chamber hidden deep in the Keep.   He removed his tunic and braes, folding them with care on top of a chest and stood in the dark chamber to let the quiet settle around him.

His tall, lithe body was tense after being around his father.   It was impossible to think clearly around Lord Invor when his father was in such a rage.   Such a strong personality and flair for the dramatic had a tendency to stir negative energies in everyone around his father.   Yet is was also that strength that held Dragonslair together in times of strife, binding all of the occupants with the common knowledge that the Lord of Dragonslair could and would protect what was his – to the death if need be.   It had taken years for Eric to learn how to combat the doubt and hurt to reach a space within for self-reflection, protecting him from the negativity in a sphere of positive vibrations.   Eric didn't blame his father for his feelings, yet the damage to father and sons was deep, causing invisible wounds, which overshadowed everything else in their lives.

Eric pulled on a luxurious royal blue robe, the stiff high, cowl-like collar encircling his neck almost concealing his ears.   He lit a candle on the large writing desk near the fireplace then poured clear oil from the earthen jar he kept on a shelf located close by, into the bowl sitting in the center of the table.   From a pouch containing powders, a mixture of herbs and incense, Eric measured the exact amount before placing them into the bowl of oil.   He touched the candle flame to the oil, a soft blue blaze engulfing the mixture to send up a sweet scent as it filled the room.   The odor relaxed his tired mind and body, his eyes following the movements of the flame.

Concentrating, Eric followed the flame's path as it wavered, slowly dwindled, and then went out altogether.

All that remained was a soft glow in the center of the oil and the slowly moving liquid in a rainbow of colors inside the bowl. A mist rose, clouding Eric's mind with emotions and images of staggering intensity. Slowly, the brilliance cleared, and he saw a large panther, sleek and strong standing guard by a door. The image of a young woman standing next to his brother took shape. She was glorious, a gleaming sword thrust out and pointed directly at Gavilan. Her essence glowed around her, engulfing both of the images in golden sunshine.

The scene changed, and Eric saw hideous looking beasts that resembled wolves, chasing Gavilan's party. There was something unworldly about the animals, but Eric wasn't sure what it was until he saw their eyes. Their eyes glowed as red as coals from a hearth, and they had unusual teeth, bared in grotesque grins unlike any earthly beasts he had ever seen or studied. He found himself trapped by the vision, unable to pull away from the repulsive evil they extruded even through his dream. Eric felt his soul lurch with the rage he saw in those eyes.

A killing rage!

Demons killing and rampaging through the countryside in possession of a living animal's body. The images switched, and Eric saw Gavilan and Laydya holding each other in a tight embrace, quietly sitting by a fire with a large fur wrapped around both of their shoulders. They were looking deep into each other's eyes, communicating in the ageless way of lovers. The novice Druid realized Gavilan had finally met his match in this woman, if his stubborn brother would just allow it!

Drained by the amount of energy it took to hold the images, Eric pushed the mist from his mind. Pulling away from the bowl with a sense of dread, he mentally searched the library for the scrolls to find some answers. He knew someone was responsible for what was going on, someone powerful enough to manipulate living flesh into doing a perverse will. Eric could only hope that Lady Laydya and Gavilan were bound close enough to endure the challenges that were coming their way. He didn't think they were going to have any choice in this unholy war.

Eric had no doubts about Gavilan's strength, but he worried about his brother's ability to accept things that were beyond this world. He knew Gavilan hated magic of any kind, be it good or evil! His only prayer was that Lady Laydya was strong enough to overcome Gavilan's bullheadedness, because they could only defeat this plague upon the land if they trusted each other completely.

As he replayed the images, another thought struck Eric. The last image of Gavilan and the girl came to mind again, and he chuckled. Yes, he had a feeling before all of this was over, Gavilan was going to learn a thing or two about magic. He recalled the demon images, and decided he needed to talk to someone from the order. There was a lingering uneasiness about those images, something familiar . . . but what?

Or Who?

Clearing away his mess, Eric began his search. The scrolls were the key, he was sure of it. Somewhere in history, he was sure someone of the order had recorded the answers, and it was waiting there for him to find it.

Chapter 4

As the three weary travelers picked their way out of the mountain pass and finally came into the bright sunlight, Gavilan was grateful that they were almost to their destination.   His spirits lifted as they crested the last rise to look down on a wide valley.   Everywhere there were coffers' huts and tilled soil, livestock grazing contentedly and people working the fields, oblivious to the horror that stalked the land on the other side of the mountain ridge.

He wondered yet again if he were doing the right thing . . bringing Laydya to Dragonslair could actually bring the danger down on their heads instead of saving her from whomever this maniac was that continually nipped at their heels. Gavilan was thankful that the rest of their journey had been unhampered by supernatural beings, because he was worried enough over Dougal's condition. Laydya did all that she could, but the warrior's strength was fading fast. If he didn't get them within the safety of Dragonslair soon, they would be burying him instead of tending his wounds. He heard a soft gasp of delight from his right as they pulled the horses to a halt.

"Behold, Dragonslair, Lady Laydya. The jewel of the western lands!"

Laydya turned as she heard the wonder and pride in his voice. He didn't look at her, but scrutinize valley below like a starving person forced to watch a feast he was forbidden to join.

"How long has it been, since you were here?" she asked, reaching out as she did so to steady Dougal's horse.   She almost missed his answer.

"Too long . . . !" he whispered without looking at her. "Come, let's get Dougal to a warm bed and a fire." Without another word, he positioned Dougal's horse between them again so they could steady the wounded warrior on the final decent to Dragonslair.

They were almost to the more populated areas when Laydya remembered she hadn't seen Damen in the last little while. He had remained unusually quiet during the last two days, keeping to the shadows of camp as if to guard them from unseen enemies. She swung her head around, searching for him, but couldn't locate the big cat. Instantly, she reached out with her senses, using invisible threads of light to locate him.

There . . . just inside the line of trees, she finally found huge beastie. A chill made Laydya cringe when she was reminded what strangers would think when and if they found him. Laydya knew all too well what the danger from these strangers to the huge cat and she could be due to superstitions and wives tales. Once these people realized she traveled with Damen it was only a matter of time that he and Laydya would be scorned and thrown out of Dragonslair as the cursed one that she was rather than some special Learned role that Lowen and Dougal were so convinced she was destined to fill.

She faltered for a moment, trying to prepare herself for the rebuke and loneliness that would come when they entered Gavilan's home. He wouldn't want to be associated with someone considered an outcast such as herself, and it would be too dangerous to bring Damen inside the protected walls of the keep. The stab of hurt caused her to visibly flinch, drawing Gavilan's attention.

"What ails you now, woman? Do you sense something from that cat?" he growled, pulling the horses up short to search her face. When she didn't answer right away, he swore, pulling his sword out and searching the area around them.

Gavilan's sharp eyes found nothing out of the ordinary,

but he had learned not to trust just his eyes. The cattle to their left seemed only mildly interested in their passing, and no fowl took flight in sudden terror. Everywhere he scanned, all looked peaceful and content. He turned back to Laydya and found tears brimming in her golden eyes.

"Laydya, you must tell me what you sense. I cannot protect you if you don't confide in me!" he snarled, clearly ready to defend them at all costs.

He watched a single tear escaped and slide down her cheek, making a watery track through the dirt and trail dust she hadn't been able to wash off since they had left the Circle of Stones. The sight of that tear tore at his chest, gripping it in a vice so strong he found it hard to breathe.

"She . . . worries . . . about the . . . cat!" came a thready sound, barely audible, from Dougal. "And . . . what your people . . . will think . . . of her!"

Shamed, Laydya bowed her head, unable to meet those emerald orbs. Now that the words were uttered, Gavilan would realize that he couldn't take her to his home. And there was no way she wouldn't leave Damen unprotected in a strange land.

Without looking up, she said, "Go, take Dougal to your home. Tend him well!" Before she could move, Gavilan was beside her, forcing her chin up to look at him.

"What did you think would happen?" he questioned, anger and rebuke clearly readable in his eyes. "Did you think I would leave both of you outside the gates after finally getting you here? Are you mad, woman?" He tore his hand away, spinning the horse on its hindquarters in anger. The next instant a high-pitched whistle echoed across the meadow, and almost exact duplicate of Laydya's when she called Damen to her.

"Noooo. . ." she screamed. "You cannot not do this! They will kill him, don't you see? Only the people of

Valeyrian tolerated him, and that was because he was raised with me. Your people will never accept him," she pleaded, pulling on the sleeve of his tunic as she tried to stop him. She would do whatever it took to keep the Damen safe. Before she could say more Damen materialized beside her, his agitation clear at being summoned by someone other than his mistress. Gavilan's anger was almost a physical presence as he turned toward her again.

"The people within those walls may be strangers, and superstitious of things that are different, Lady Laydya. But, they will accept you and that black demon cat of yours if I tell them to! It isn't safe outside the keep, and I know you will not leave him behind. So, there is no other choice. He comes in, just as you do!" Emerald eyes warred with golden ones, and it was Laydya who was forced to turn away first.

"So be it, warrior!" she swore out loud. "But you may regret it, for I have first-hand knowledge of how people react to things they don't understand! You," she added, her eyes still bright with unshed tears, "have no idea what can happen. There is no way you can force people to accept things they don't understand. I know . . . I have spent my life trying!" With those profound words hanging between them, she grabbed the lead to Dougal's horse and nudged her to move down the trail.

It took Gavilan a moment to control his anger and realize that she had conceded to his command. However, it was the meaning of her last words that finally softened his anger. Since he had joined this ragged group of misfits, Gavilan had fought the odd feelings that had surfaced from time to time toward this strange young woman who seem to change before his eyes.

One minute she was an aloof, spoiled heiress who was convinced she was the "Chosen" from legends of old, and the next a temptress gazing at him with honey-colored eyes flicked with bronze so like those of her feline friend.   Her temper was almost a match for his own, and the thought made him grin.   Never before had he met any woman who would stand toe to toe against him in an argument.   Nor had any female dare raise a sword to challenge him, much less actually fight him.   He was quickly realizing that there was much more to Lady Laydya Valeyrian than met the eye.

Gavilan kneed his mount to catch up with the tiresome enchantress who seem to fill way too much of his thoughts lately, vowing to discover the many facets of the woman who rode in front of him.   If he was going to become further involved in this outrageous plot of hers, he was determined to discover as much about her as possible before continuing on this quest.   He couldn't think of a safer place to do so for the moment than his father's Keep.

As they reached the outskirts of the Keep, Laydya chose to slide from her horse lead Dougal's with Damen close at her side.   Gavilan rode close to Dougal, making sure the horses didn't spook as people came out from their huts to stare at the girl garbed in men's clothes, a sword at her waist and a huge black cat calmly walking like a shadow by her side.

Laydya held her head high.   She could see the familiar looks in their eyes.   Fear,   rebuke and curiosity!   Laydya refused to bow her head, instead following Gavilan's horse, unwilling to allow their opinions and fears to touch her mind.   If Gavilan wouldn't listen to her, then he would have to experience it the hard way.   She only hoped that no one would get hurt in the process.

As they entered the main gates and finally the outer courtyards, Gavilan could feel the stares of so many people on them, and his anger returned.   He kept silent until they reached the gates of the inner courtyard where he was forced to dismount.   Turning to the throng of people who had followed them, he raised both hands in an appeal for quiet.

"This is Lady Laydya Valeyrian and her Master-at-Arms, who has been wounded.   The beast you see next to her is Damen.   He is the Lady's pet, and tame for the most part." Gavilan drilled all of them with his hard stare, daring any to voice objections.   "I have offered them the protection of Dragonslair, so I beg of you to make them welcome."   His booming voice hung over the crowd, and it was several heartbeats before anyone made a sound.   Then, like a wave, they all yelled and smiled, acknowledging his command.

Gavilan turned toward Laydya to see her standing there pale and stiff with Damen next to her.   She had her hand buried in the fur of his neck, as if to steady herself or possibly to keep the cat in place.

"I told you," he leaned down to whisper softly into her ear.   He gently pried each finger of her hand from the death grip she had Damen's ruff and pulled it to his lips to kiss. "They may not understand all of it, but there will be no trouble."

Laydya couldn't find the words to say thank you.   She knew he had done it so she would feel safe, but the manner in which he had accomplished it numbed her mind.   As if he were a royal king, Gavilan had commanded, and the people had accepted his word.   Just like that!

"Lowen . . . told you . . . to trust . . . him!" came Dougal's pain filled words, just before he slid unconscious from his horse.

"Dougal!" she screamed, lunging to catch him before he hit the ground.   The old warrior's massive weight was caught by tender hands that beat her to him, and she turned to see Gavilan's eyes only inches from her own.

"We need to get him inside, so Eric can tend him. Bring the packs, I'll get someone to help me carry him."

Motioning for one of the large guards, Laydya could only stand by and watch as her old friend was tenderly carried into the inner courtyard, disappearing around the corner out of sight.

She didn't wait to make sense of it all, but grabbed the herbal pouches and other packs. With a silent hand signal, Laydya motioned Damen to follow. The huge cat paused for just a moment in the entrance of the courtyard and looked back at the people gaping at him. He let out an irritated hiss before following his mistress.

Chapter 5

It was late before Gavilan managed to convince Laydya to seek the bedchamber the little maid had shown her and rest. Dougal was finally resting quietly in a spacious chamber next to hers where she could hear him if need be, and Eric had been sent for. Gavilan had made no mention to his father's whereabouts, and Laydya was too tired at the moment to care.

As soon as she entered the suite of rooms that had been given to her, Laydya's exhaustion caught up with her. Damen lay near the hearth, his eyes reflecting the light of the flames that was the only heat in the room. She walked over and knelt beside him, leaning her tired head on his massive neck.

"I hope I have not led both of us to our own destruction, my friend. I'm so tired of fighting, I just wish for some peace." As if understanding her every word, the cat rubbed his head against her shoulder, his deep purr filling the room. Laydya rose and surveyed the chamber, too tired to appreciate its opulence.

A large bed against the wall beckoned to her, but she was determined to at least wash some of the grime off her person before climbing between the blankets that looked so inviting. She was about to pull her tunic over her head when there was knock on the door, and then it opened. Two young men struggled with a portable bathing tub that they placed before the roaring hearth, all the while keeping a leery eye on the huge monster that refused to move when they entered. As soon as they backed out of the door without a word, two women came in carrying buckets of hot water. It took several trips but in no time, a hot steam rose from the tub. The steam invited Laydya to soak her tired body in its misty depths. She could only stare as the last of the hot water was poured into it, dumbfounded and touched by the kindness. One of the women stood next to the tub, waiting to assist her, but Laydya was too embarrassed.

"Thank you," Laydya whispered to the woman, who blushed profusely. "You need not stay to help me. I have been attending myself for a long time now. I think I can manage, but I appreciate you offer."

"But my lady, the young master ordered me to stay until you retired to your bed. He would not like it if I shirked my duties." The older woman was terrified to look Laydya in the eye, but she watched Damen like the cat would jump her at any second. Her hands were trembling as she held out a large drying cloth meant for Laydya to disrobe. She could sense the woman's terror, and felt sorry for her. Those of her own home were uneasy around Damen, so how could expect a perfect stranger not to be terrified by his presence.

"Go," she whispered kindly. "I'll not tell Gavilan you left. I just need some time alone."

The maid bobbed her head and backed out the door, all the while keeping her eye on the black monster by the fire. As soon as the door closed, Laydya's shoulders slumped.

"See what you do to people, you big tease! That poor woman almost rattled her old bones apart because of you." Damen only yawned, showing how worried he was about the whole thing. She grinned for the first time that day.

In short order, Laydya was soaking in the hot water up to her chin. Her hair felt clean for the first time in days. Closing her eyes, she leaned back against the rim of the tub and let the rose scented water ease tired muscles too long on the trail, and soften the chafed skin on inner thighs rough from long hours in the saddle. The wound in her arm was almost a memory, and as Laydya looked down at it, she was amazed there wasn't a scar. The Druidess' healing was renowned throughout Valeyrian, but this was the first time Laydya had experienced to this extent. It had healed quicker than normal, causing a pang of guilt and sorrow to wash over her. Exhaustion and grief sapped what little strength she had left, and the warmth of the water soon lulled Laydya into an exhausted slumber as she soaked in the tub.

That was how Gavilan found her when he decided to make sure she was settled properly. With no answer to his knock, he gently opened the door and looked at the bed. Seeing it empty he was about to go looking for her when a movement next to the hearth drew his attention. Damen lay next to the bathing tub with his head resting on his paws, but his eyes watched every move Gavilan made. It took a moment for the warrior to realize that someone was in the tub, and his heart skipped a beat.

She lay there with her hair washed and hanging over the rim so it could dry, the water coming up to her neck. Gavilan quietly moved to stand next to the tub and gazed down on the young woman who had turned his world upside down in a matter of days. He could almost make out her womanly curves beneath the murky water, and could clearly see her breasts from his vantage point.

Rosy tips invited his fingertips to touch, to tease them into standing at attention just for him. Her breath was even and deep, and he realized that she had fallen asleep and would drown if he left her there.

Gavilan bent down to kneel next to the tub and gently touched her chin in a caress, not really meaning to but doing so all the same. Laydya's sleepy response was almost his undoing. She opened those expressive eyes and looked up at him with an innocent smile before closing them once again. He continued to look his fill at her until it dawned on him she was fast asleep again.

"Well, my friend," he whispered to the big cat who had come to sit next to him. "I guess I had better take your mistress out of the water before she catches her death." With those profound words, Gavilan rose and turned down the bed covers. He arranged the pillows and picked up the drying cloth, in a quandary as to how to accomplish his mission without waking her. There was really no way to avoid it, so, he flung the cloth over his shoulder and reached under the water to scoop the lady up in his wet arms.

As he stood, Laydya let out a sigh, but otherwise remained blissfully unaware of what was happening. He stood gazing down at her, marveling at the beauty that had been so completely hidden beneath the leathers, tunic and boots she had worn on the trail. His body quickly reminded Gavilan that he had to get her dried and in bed before he complete dishonored himself. He sat in a large chair next to the hearth and wrapped the drying cloth around her.

With gentle fingers, he fanned her long hair out so the heat of the flames could finish drying it, all the while gently rubbing the linen cloth over her wet body. It was some time before he felt her hair was dry enough so that she wouldn't take a chill during the night. Reluctantly, Gavilan laid her on the turned down bed sheets and covered her. He searched for Damen, and found him sprawled out on the floor beside the bed. Anyone entering the room would not see him until it was too late.

"Guard her well, my friend." He didn't realize he had spoken out loud until the cat's hiss echoed in the quiet room. Gavilan stoked the fire so that it would not die out during the early morning hours, and went seeking his own bed. It had been a long day, and there was still his father to face in the morning!

Chapter 6

Loud, angry voices were what finally led Laydya to the great hall the next morning. After rising late and checking on Dougal, she had been certain everyone would be busy with the day's chores. Instead, she entered quietly, choosing a small alcove by the stairs to remain out of sight. No one in the hall took notice of her. Gavilan was heatedly arguing with another man, older and similar in height and bearing, but not in appearance. Where Gavilan's hair was long and dark with a tendency to curl at the nape of his neck when damp, the other man's hair was straight and reddish blonde. They shared the same color of eyes, though! And at the moment, both sets of eyes were filled with anger.

"What do you mean, you've brought her here? Do you have any idea what kind of danger you have brought down on our heads? Was it not enough that you jeopardize Eric's safety by getting yourself taken prisoner, causing him to run off and think he could save you? Oh no, you have to bring that devil woman to *my* home, and expect me to protect her along with that monster cat she travels with!"

Gagel Invor's ire was evident, for he stood facing his powerfully built son without a thought of the damage Gavilan could inflict on him if he so chose. Never for a moment had Gagel ever feared his son, nor did he now. Yet he could sense the barely leashed fury beneath the surface, and secretly admired this son who refused to bend to anyone.

"Sire," Gavilan broke in, his anger just as evident. "There is no reason for you to worry, at least not right now. The threat didn't follow us through the pass. If Dougal is to be believed, it cannot leave Valeyrian lands . . . at least not yet." Gavilan watched as his father began pacing again, reminding Gavilan of Damen's restlessness when they were within the Circle of Stones.   His thoughts were interrupted by Gagel's finger poking his chest just a little too hard.

"You had better hope that this Dougal is correct. What of Dragonslair?   How do we protect it from this madman you say cannot be destroyed?   Huh?   Answer me that!"   Gagel stood, hands fisted on his hips, waiting for an answer Gavilan didn't have.

"There is no way to protect your home if Kasadim decides to take it.   I know, for I watched as mine was destroyed before my eyes!"   Laydya's voice echoed from the alcove, causing the two men to turn toward it in surprise.

She stepped into the great hall and stood before them dressed in clean leggings and tunic, her sword at her waist. Thankful she had taken the time to braid her hair,   Laydya couldn't meet Gavilan's eyes after realizing it had been he who had put her to bed last night.   The thought made her body flush hot from head to toe, but she stood her ground. It was not Gavilan's fault that they were being hounded at every turn by this lunatic.   She refused to allow him to take any more of his father's abuse.

"So, you must be Lady Laydya Valeyrian."   Gagel's familiar-looking eyes took in her appearance with something close to disgust before turning to his son once more. "What do you plan to do now?   Leave her here while you go off looking for this Kasadim yourself?"

"He isn't going alone, if he chooses to go at all," Laydya answered for Gavilan before he had a chance to open his mouth.   "This is my journey, not your son's."

Gagel pounced on her like a bird of prey, towering over her like a hawk ready to strike.   "So, you answer for him as well.   What spell have you worked on Gavilan that causes him to go against his natural instincts and protect you?"

She almost cowered at his massive presence, until she reached out and mentally touched his hurt.   Deep within,

Laydya felt the rage of a father who felt betrayed, a man who had loved a son so completely that he would have done anything to save him. But now, the pain of that betrayal tore these two apart, reopening old wounds. She pulled back into herself, shivering at the intensity of the feelings emanating from a proud father who had lost so much.

"No spell could force your son to go against his beliefs, Lord Invor. You of all people should know this. Gavilan chose to help us, as an honorable man. If he doesn't wish to continue the journey, no one will blame him, nor can he blame himself."

Keeping her tone soft and feminine, Laydya projected a sense of peace and harmony toward Gagel, trying to soothe the fragile edges of his presence without his sensing it. When she saw him visibly relax, she took a deep breath, not realizing she had been holding it. Someone materialize beside her, and Laydya felt the feather-light touch of someone gifted reaching out to her.

"You did well, my lady. My father is a formidable man when in a rage, but you used your gift to ease his hurt pride and guilt. It was well done of you!" Surprised by the compliment and the "touch" she turned to find a stunningly handsome young man about her own age standing behind her.

"I am Eric, brother to Gavilan," he added, this time for all to hear.

"Stop sneaking up on people, Eric! It unnerves them," Gagel said in disgust before throwing up his hands and stalking out of the room. Everyone flinched when they heard the heavy outside door slam shut behind him.

"Well brother, it seems that it didn't take long for things to return to normal." Eric's grin caused Gavilan to frown. "And you, my lady! I've never seen a woman stand up to our father as you did. Many would cower at his menacing presence, especially when he is as angry as he is now. You are truly a remarkable woman!"

Laydya flushed, trying hard to avoid looking at Gavilan but she could not do so for long. She almost jumped when he appeared inches from her nose, his stormy eyes almost black with anger.

"Why did you interfere?" he shouted directly into her face, causing Laydya to visibly flinch.

"Well excuse me, my lord!" she hissed, now unwilling to feel any embarrassment from the night. "I *thought* you would appreciate my taking your side! You were just standing there, allowing him to vent that rubbish on you when it wasn't your fault. Remind me next time to hand him an ax so he can lop off you head!"

Without hesitation, Laydya pushed pass the brothers and went in search of her rooms. It was time to take Damen out to hunt, and get some fresh air. The confines of the Keep were suddenly too restrictive for her own good.

"Now look what you've done!" Eric whispered, shaking his head.

"What do you mean, what I've done? She needs to learn to keep that mouth of her's shut!" Gavilan growled over his shoulder as he storming out of the room after her.

Left alone in the empty hall, Eric wondered if it was healthy to allow the two of them to go off together, and then decided not to intercede. It was better to let nature take its course. After all, they hadn't harmed one another - yet.

Still, he felt uneasy, knowing his brother as he did. Eric had felt the tender core of emotions Laydya concealed from the world, and if Gavilan wasn't careful, he could do irreparable damage. He only hoped his brother would bend to the call of nature that pulled these two together, otherwise, Eric feared for the lady's survival. At the reminder of Laydya's quest, Eric remembered an old document he had seen in the library and decided now was as good a time as any to dig it out.   He had a feeling that there would be no peace around the keep in the days to come.

Chapter 7

Laydya was thinking the same thing as she and Damen made their way toward a grove of trees outside the safety of the keep walls. Forced to saddle her own horse because the stable boy had been too terrified to move when he had seen Damen, she had sent the cat out the gates and returned for her mount. Now she let the warm afternoon sun soothe her frayed nerves and ease the tension in her neck. She needed to practice and Laydya knew she couldn't do that inside the Keep walls.

Once inside the concealing line of trees, the forest sounds eased the last bit of tension, and allowed Laydya to think more clearly. No wonder Gavilan and his father didn't get along, they were too much alike. Maybe not in appearance, but in all other manner they were alike. Such strong temperaments, the determination of warriors and leaders, and stubborn! Gods, she knew that all too well.

Damen's hiss caught her attention, and Laydya grinned down at the ebony cat whose eyes gleamed in the defused light under the thick canopy of trees.

"Go . . . find your meal and leave me in peace." She laughed out loud as he gave a kittenish swipe of a huge paw to the air before bounding out of sight. She only hoped there were no poachers' snares nearby. Feeling better, she dismounted in a clearing and tied the horse.

Shafts of sunlight filtered down from the treetops, causing fairy-like motes to dance on the soft breeze. Laydya marveled at the stillness caused by her intrusion, settling down on a stump to take in the peace and quiet. Slowly, the normal sounds of the forest returned . . . the call of birds, the chattering of squirrels and somewhere close by wild geese honked.

Finally allowing the peace to sink into her very fibers,

she stood and drew her sword.   The sound of steel rang loud and strong in the clearing as it left the scabbard, and Laydya stepped into the dance with practiced ease.   She was oblivious to anything around her, knowing that if danger approached, Damen wasn't far way.

Gavilan found her thus, and kept his distance as he watched her repeat the drill over and over.   He was amazed when she inserted several kicks and jumps that accentuated her long legs, reminding him that Dougal had trained this wisp of a girl to defend herself against almost any opponent. He was convinced Laydya would never be able to defend herself against a truly aggressive man, but in most fights Gavilan was sure she could at least do some serious harm.

As he continued to watch, Laydya lay down the sword and began to execute a strange, dance-like set of maneuvers that were as graceful as any dancer Gavilan had ever seen. Each step was symmetrically connected to the last, the muscles of her legs and arms flexible and strong.

He was reminded of her nude form the night before. The muscled texture of her legs and torso, and his body reacted instantly.   He forced the memory of rosebud tipped breasts from his mind, and struggled for control over his body's long denied needs.

A movement from his left caught Gavilan's attention, and Damen appeared, licking his lips.   The big cat settled in the shade of a bush and began cleaning his paws, keeping a protective eye on his mistress and her watcher.   Assured that Laydya was in no danger, Gavilan decided to return to the keep.   There were things needing his attention.   There was also the matter of his sire!   Somehow, he was determined to make Gagel understand the danger was not just for Laydya's lands, but for everyone's.   The problem was, how to accomplish it!

Chapter 8

Laydya hadn't seen Gavilan for two days. She tried to find other things to keep busy, not let it drive her crazy but the stupid man kept sneaking into her thoughts at the oddest times. Whenever she asked about him, all she was told was he was about Dragonslair business but no one would give her exact directions. This morning she'd had enough and cornered the little maid who was assigned to her chambers.

"Have you seen Gavilan?" Laydya spoke softly to the timid miss who was changing the bed linens as she sat in the corner cleaning several of her blades. Watching from the corner of her eye she knew the young woman heard her when there was a slight hitch in the way the maid brushed the top quilts into place.

"Malady, the young Sir has been busy." The maid continued as if nothing else was needed.

"Yes, that seems to be the general comment each time I try to find him." She hated intimidating the young woman but Eric had been missing for several days after making sure she was settled. Gavilan was in the wings his father refused to even speak to her most of the time. Laydya's famous temper was close to the boiling point. The young maid finished her tasks and hustled out of the so fast it had Laydya shaking her head and a quiet laugh bubbling up for the first time in a long time.

So, the man was avoiding her.

She had been spending most of her time with either Dougal or Eric, Laydya tried to stay as invisible as possible and ensuring Dougal's wounds healed. Everywhere she turned, Laydya felt eyes upon her but could never locate just who it was that followed. The atmosphere of the keep was one of open hostility and fear as servants scattered each time she entered a room, and no one would enter her bed chamber except the a maid that Eric assigned. Everyone was terrified of a black monster cat that slept next to his mistress.

Rumors and sneers could be heard as servants covered their mouths, fearing she could put some sort of spell on them. It wasn't anything Laydya hadn't experienced before from her own people but she thought she was finally immune. At one point the devilish streak in her was just too much, and she deliberately stared at an old woman who refused to let her out of her sight.

Laydya had been in the kitchens, looking for something to hold off her hunger until the evening meal. Lately, it seem she was always hungry, but today it had been worse than usual. The servant had continued to shadow her every step all morning, and Laydya had had enough.

"What?" she screamed, turning on the woman. "Do you want me to give you two heads and the body of a toad?" she shouted, throwing her hands up high over her head in semblance of a demon. The poor woman shrieked and threw her apron over her head, before running headlong out of the room. Laydya almost laughed at the sight, until she saw Gavilan leaning against the entrance of the kitchens. Instantly contrite, she refused to say a word to him or apologize for her behavior, opting to leave before he could vent his anger on her. It was the last time she had seen him. It was no wonder he didn't want anything to do with her.

Gavilan had watched the entire scene between Laydya and the old woman as he stood in the shadows. He could tell from her walk Lady Laydya Valeyrian was very near the end of her temper. He watched her stalk off after the incident offering no word because if he did Gavilan was sure he would lose what little control he had and burst out laughing. He had entered the kitchens just in time to hear Laydya's words, and see the reaction of the servant. That anyone could think this mere slip of a woman was more than what she seemed was beyond his understanding. There wasn't a mean bone in her body, yet he wasn't oblivious to how the servants and others were treating her.

Then why haven't you stepped in and put a stop to it? His conscious nagged him, mentally kicking his own ass.

He no idea how to make them see what he did, the sweet core of femininity hidden beneath boyish leathers and tunics, tall riding books. That she refused to dress as the Lady of Valeyrian Keep wasn't lost on him, but it might have helped ease some of the problems with his people. But not Laydya. No, she was determined to be who and what she was no matter what those around her thought of her and it made him respect her just a little bit more.

Damn, he needed to talk to his father. Letting out a sigh, Gavilan went in search of his father.

It was chaos when Laydya entered the great hall for the midday meal. She had intended to slip into the kitchens and just grab something to eat and a snack for Damen, then leave by the side doors. But the pandemonium coming from the near the large central hearth where the family usually convened drew her inside the hall. It shouldn't have surprised her at all, seeing Gavilan and his father toe to toe again. Yet this time, it seemed there was more determination by both men to have the last word. She saw Eric standing out of the way, and slipped over to join him.

"What do they fight about this time? Me?" she whispered, keeping her voice pitched low so as not to be noticed. Laydya didn't want to be accused of taking sides yet again.

"No, but it could be just a bad. Father doesn't understand the danger, and Gavilan cannot accept that Kasadim cannot be stopped by an army. I'm afraid they will never agree on anything as long as they don't speak of what really is at the heart of all this anger."

Eric didn't need to explain further. Laydya could sense the emotions of both men as they raged at each other, their shouts echoing off the rafters high above like two bulls locked in mortal combat. Suddenly Lord Ivor advanced on his older son, standing face to face, shouting for all to hear.

"You have been a disappointment and bane to my existence since the day you were born. How could a sweet, kind woman such as your mother ever have given birth to one such as you?"

Stunned silence filled the room for a moment, and the look on Gavilan's face broke Laydya's heart. She could sense the violence in him, and almost stepped forward, but Eric stopped her. Gavilan's reaction was unexpected, and indeed violent. He turned and brought his huge forearm down onto the solid wood mantel above the hearth with so much force it shuddered first, then split in half. The two massive pieces hung for a heartbeat before thudding to the stone hearth below. He didn't say a word to his sire, but as glaring green eyes met surprised emerald ones, both men knew that each had gone too far and said too much. Gavilan turned and stormed from the room, leaving all to stare at the broken mantel. As Laydya watched, Gagel slumped into his chair and leaned back with closed eyes. The Lord of Dragonslair looked as if he had aged ten years in just a matter of minutes.

"Go find Gavilan, my lady. Make him talk to you. Whatever it takes, the two of them must come together, or all will be lost!" Tears threatened the handsome young man's eyes as he turned to Laydya, silently pleading for his family.

"But what can I do? He won't listen to me half the time. Indeed, we argue almost as bad as the two of them do." Laydya searched for a reason to follow Gavilan, but it was Eric's pleading eyes that finally convinced her. "I'll try, that is all I can promise."

Eric grinned, silently reaching out to her with his

"touch." *"Get him to take you to his special place. Few have ever gone near it, thinking it is enchanted. Go with him, my lady. He needs you now more than ever right now!"*

Laydya's nape tingled as he withdrew, leaving her feeling bewildered and uncertain. As she stood looking at Eric, she knew there was no choice in the matter. Turning, she called Damen to her, but Eric stopped her.

"Leave your protector with me. You won't have no need of him with Gavilan."

She turned to once again stare at him, this time with Damen at his feet. The cat looked content as Laydya watched Eric stroke his ears, something few strangers were willing or able to do.

Without another word Laydya left the great hall in search of the angry warrior, stopping by the kitchens to grab bread, cheese and some leftover meat. She threw them into a cloth sack along with a flask of wine, and went in search of Gavilan. At the stables, she was told he had left the Keep, riding bareback on one of his father's stallions. In minutes, Laydya was saddled and using her senses to stretch out on unseen threads of light so she could find him.

Chapter 9

Amazingly, it wasn't difficult, really. She *connected* to his aura without hesitation, and followed it into the forest like a beacon of light drawing her steadily to him. Laydya found him in a grove of thick oaks with brambles and low brush all around. He was letting his mount pick its way through the thick underbrush when he suddenly pulled to a stop. As she guided her mount next to his, Laydya felt the anger and violence dissipate, replaced by the raw emotions of a little boy who felt he had been abandoned without cause. It tore at her heart, making her ache with the injustice of it all.

She, who had lived with the stigma of her birth, was use to the stares and superstitions of others around her. But this strong warrior, who refused to be beaten or enslaved, was brought low by the stubbornness of his parent who couldn't admit that he had been wronged. And what was so apparent to Laydya was the two of them were so alike.

"Why did you follow me, woman? Surely Dougal needs your tender attentions. I do not!" he hissed, much like Damen did when in a sniff. Laydya almost grinned at the image, but caught herself.

"Eric said you had special place that few would venture. Take me there, Gavilan," she whispered softly. "I have need of such a place right now." She reached out her senses, trying to soothe his hurt by letting him feel that she was no threat.

Her plea, so innocently asked, caught him off guard. He stared at her for several heartbeats, wondering yet again how so many could feel threatened by this woman with honeyed hair and unusual eyes. He couldn't find the words to explain how he felt, so he kneed the horse to continue, allowing her to follow.

If Laydya hadn't found Gavilan, she was certain she would never have found the path. Indeed, there was no path at all to the human eye. It was just a small animal trail that Gavilan seem to know by heart and see in his own mind's eye.

After picking their way through thick brambles, around huge trees, allowing the horses to pick their way down a steep, winding ravine, they emerged into a grotto that took her breath away. It reminded her of the dream she had after fleeing Valeyrian Keep, and the memory brought a wrenching ache to her chest.

A waterfall tumbled down from a height off the plateau above, giving evidence that they must have been slowly descending along the path. A mist floated up from the surface of the lake below, its scent filled with the aroma of flowers and minerals as it steeped in warm splendor beneath the sun overhead. She must have gasp at the sight, for it was Gavilan who broke the silence.

"I see you like my hide-a-way." His voice was filled with reverence for this place, so pristine and untouched by man. "When I was a boy, I would come here alone often. No one would dare follow me, since all thought that spirits protected the place. It was a perfect sanctuary," he stopped, realizing he was about to say too much.

"There is a place at Valeyrian, at least there used to be, before the attack.   It's near the lake, out of sight of the Keep and normal traffic. Lowen told me that once there stood a temple on the island at its center, where ancient priests held ceremonies for the winter and summer solstice." The memory of her homemade Laydya ache for those lost times, bringing tears to her eyes.

"I never really appreciated any of it until now." She sat on her horse, silently wondering if she would ever see her home again.

"Well," Gavilan said, breaking the long silence. "Now that you are here, what did you bring in that sack you're clutching so tightly?" He grinned as she looked down at her hand, realizing she had completely forgotten the food.

"Something to fill the belly!" she countered with a grin of her own. "I'm always hungry lately, and I thought to share some of my stolen booty with you if you ask nicely!" Laydya slid from her mount and dropped the reins, sure the animals wouldn't leave the glen. She looked around and found a large flat boulder near the water, and sat down to spread out their meal. When Gavilan crouched down beside her, Laydya almost flinched from the turmoil she sensed in him.

"Tell me why you followed me? Did that interfering brother of mine send you?" He stretched out across from her on the rock crossing those long legs, propping his head up on his hand. Gavilan watched the play of emotions that were so plain on her face, wondering which truth she would eventually choose to tell him.   He was surprised by her honesty.

"There is no reason not to tell you, I guess." She shrugged, not meeting his penetrating gaze. "Eric worries about this battle between you and your father. He doesn't want to be heir, and wants nothing to do with the running of Dragonslair. He would just as soon study his days away as not!"

"So, you came because he asked you to?" He waited, slowly munching on a piece of cheese as she fidgeted with some bread.

"I. . .   would have come on my own, if I was sure you wanted me here." With that out in the open, Laydya finally raised her eyes to meet his. She saw surprise, and something more, but what she wasn't sure.

"For some reason, I think you feel I don't approve of you. You are so wrong, my Lady," he said softly, forgetting the cheese in his hand.

"Am I?"   Laydya's breath stopped in her throat, unable

to believe that this man could see any more of what she was than strangers did.

Like a dream, she watched as his long arm reached out and cupped the back of her head, drawing her toward him. As he pulled her near, Laydya was drawn to the fullness of his lips, noticing a small scar on the side of his chin, and the wrinkles near his eyes that gave away his penchant for laughing. Odd, but she hadn't heard him laugh that much since they had met. It was her last coherent thought for some time.

Gavilan pulled her toward him with slow, deliberate pressure, afraid if he pulled to quickly she would fly away. He felt no resistance as her face drew closer, and his eyes feasted on those lips he had wanted to kiss since her first night in his home.   Now he was determined to take his pleasure with them, exploring their depths at his leisure.   When she was finally close enough for him to taste the very air she breathed, he groaned and took what he had only dreamed of

To his surprise, she tasted of the spiced wine she had just sipped, of the honeyed bread that now lay untouched on the rock beside them. He pulled her closer, drawing her on top of him as he lay back on the ground so both hands could explore. Suddenly it dawned on Gavilan that she hadn't made a move to touch him, and he forced himself to pull away and look up at her. There was a bemused expression on her face, as if she were a dreamer just awakened. When he pulled her back down to him, Lady Laydya Valeyrian became all that Gavilan could ever hope for,

He explored her mouth, his large hands mapping her slender body and hips slowly and with purpose always aware that this person in his arms was rare and worthy. So many emotions flooded her senses it was almost too much to breathe but hey, breathing was overrated at this point.

So Gavilan just continued to plunder the lush mouth he held over him, allowing her to move as she wanted and always aware of her hands. He knew he was a big man, and the one thing Gavilan didn't want to do was terrify Laydya by pushing. Easy and slow, he allowed her to set the pace even as his body tried to push the issues and his raging lust. This woman was everything he had ever wanted and at the moment the fact that she had a quest to finish, they had a monster to find, and were in the midst of a fight to save both of their homes was briefly pushed to the background. All he could think of was just how warm and wonderful it felt to hold her.

Chapter 10

She was drowning.

Laydya's first coherent thought wasn't for air when Gavilan pulled away and looked at her. Her senses were bombarded by rampant male sexuality as it assaulted her fragile grasp on her own intense emotions. Heat flushed throughout her body, causing an odd aching to begin low in her belly and radiate outward. When he pulled her back toward him for another kiss, Laydya gave in to the urges that she had only dared hope for in her dreams.

She touched the small scar on his chin, another nick on his neck, marveling at the strength of corded muscles rippling under her fingertips. When he captured her lips once more, Laydya was lost. Gavilan rolled her beneath him and she could feel the bulge that was impossible for him to hide. She groaned, arching toward the heat of him, mindlessly reaching out on those thin tentacles of light to feel him mentally as well as physically for the joining she so desperately craved. She felt his teeth toy with a rosy nipple hidden beneath her thin tunic, causing the aching to ratchet up even higher with each teasing stroke of his tongue to soak the material covering it. Heedless of the consequences, her hands worked the ties holding the front of her tunic to allow him closer. She needed skin, needed to feel his hands on her heated flesh.

There were stars . . . Laydya would have sworn the bright grotto had gone dark as stars exploded in before her closed eyes. She felt the strength of him flow through her, and savored his taste, the purely male scent of this warrior who held her securely in his massive arms. Her drugged mind lost contact with reality as he continued his gentle assault on her body and mind, and Laydya gave in to the onslaught.

He was lost! There was no other explanation for his loss of control Gavilan usually managed to maintain when with a woman. Laydya's innocent response to his touch drove all rational thought from his brain, leaving him with a need to be skin to skin with another woman as soon as possible. He was barely aware of her tearing the ties of her tunic loose, only pulling his head down to suckle at her breasts in raptured delight. The small, throaty sounds she made drove him on. His only goal was to take the moaning woman in his arms to the highest peak as she begged him to hold her closer.

"Easy, kitten. There is time," he cooed over her heated nipple, blowing on it to feel the vibrations shake her entire body. He gently stroked the silken skin of her belly, feeling her automatically push into his palm in mindless abandon. He chuckled and took the other nipple in his mouth to give it the same attention he had bestowed on the other. Gavilan felt her shudder, her strong arms contracting around his shoulders as she drew him closer.

There was no way he could release her now that he had her in his arms. He wanted to show her the stars, teach her the song of lovers as he worshipped Laydya's body honed by hours of practice and use to riding a horse as well as any man. How could this woman who was so innocent be so wanton and call to his soul at the same time.

"We've got to stop now," he growled, breathing hard and fast as if he had just conquered an army alone.

Laydya managed to focus on him, and it took a moment for her to realize he had stopped. She reached up to gently touch his face, touched by his willpower. "Don't you dare stop, warrior," she whispered.

"I know what I do now. Please, don't deny me . . . it may be the last chance I ever have to experience this kind of pleasure, and I would have it be you!"

Tears sparkled in her tawny eyes, and one escaped from her dark lashes to trek down the side of her check. Gavilan reached down and caught it on the tip of his finger, bringing it to his lips as if in a trance. She watched him war with himself, unsure who would win this particular battle . . . the knight sworn to protect the innocent, or the lover who devoured her now with his eyes. When he hissed and swore in a language even she didn't know, Laydya knew she had won.

"Come here minx!" he hissed again, gathering her to him as he once more plundered her lips.

It was Laydya's turn to tear at his clothes. She needed to feel the heat of him next to her skin more than the air she needed, needed to feel the raw power of this warrior who was both hypnotic and terrifying to her. It didn't take either of them long to shed their remaining clothing, and soon skin touched skin, unhindered by exterior trappings. She marveled at the rough texture of him as she kissed each scar on his torso, pushing him onto his back so she could look down at him. Her hands explored the feel of him, relishing his responses each time she brushed close to his inner thigh. When he grabbed her hand the next time she came too close to his swollen sex, Laydya's startled eyes met his.

"Don't tempt the dragon, my lady. Not unless you want me to embarrass both of us." He took the sting out of his words by grinning at her, and Laydya smiled.

"Now, it is my turn to tease the hare!" he goaded her, flipping her beneath him with a twist of his stronger body.

His hands worshiped everywhere his imagination had taken him in the long, dark nights since he had last seen her in the bath. Each valley, each molding of her hips, all were lay bare before his eyes to explore. In the end, it was Laydya who finally cried out for release as his lips took what no man had ever touched. His head rested against her woman's mound, her arousal strong and heady as he looked up her strong body as their eyes connected. Gavilan didn't give her time to panic or think. His long tongue flicked out and licked across the sensitive crown of her clit and took his first taste of her.

He held her hips down as Laydya cried out as he took his fill, his tongue like a sword as it speared deep and long into her folds to lick every drop of dew from her leaking channel. Tremors shook her slender frame until a sheen glistened over her entire body and Gavilan could tell Laydya was falling apart.

Gavilan rose to his knees and gazed down at the perfection of the woman laid out before him. He slipped one of his large fingers into her heated channel and felt heaven clench his fingers, tight and wet. He could just envision that tightness wrapped around his cock and he nearly lost it. She was so small, so tight he was afraid of hurting her.

"Please . . ." he watched her beg, not really knowing what it was she ached for. She twisted beneath him, her body begging for release and he could feel the slight push from her senses entwine with his to swamp both of them in intense pleasure.

Watching her face, Gavilan added a second finger and pushed both just a little deeper, spreading them to open Laydya's untried passage and hopefully make it easier for her first time. He had always avoided virgins and the thought of Laydya's virginity was almost his undoing.

"There will be some pain the first time," he gasp, trying to hold onto his control just a little longer. When she didn't answer, Gavilan realized she was beyond listening.

Placing his swollen shaft at her entrance, he slowly entered her, and almost died of pleasure as her tight passage gripped him. Withdrawing to the tip, he slowly entered again, coming up against the thin membrane that proved she was innocent. Gavilan almost stopped upon feeling that barrier, realizing that to pass it would change their lives forever.

Laydya felt his hesitation, and took matters into her own hands. Tightening her legs around him, she arched up as she pulled him down to her with legs made strong by hours of practice and riding. At the same time, she used her arms to pull herself up to his head and captured his lips.

Gavilan lost the battle with his body as he felt her muscles contract around him, pulling him even deeper than before. He watched as the woman beneath him found her pleasure through his half-closed lids. He thrust hard, burying himself deep and felt her hold him hot and deep within her body and Gavilan knew he had found home. He continued to move and tried to make sure Laydya was riding her own pleasure as he took his own. The familiar tingling at the base of his spine shot straight to his ball and there was no holding back. Throwing back his head, he roared as he felt himself penetrate her all the way to her womb.

He felt Laydya shudder beneath him, her breathing ragged with sobs as she clung to his shoulders, her short nails digging into his back. Collecting himself, Gavilan braced himself on top of her and brushed the hair from her face, kissing the tears that coursed down her cheeks.

"You shouldn't have taken matters into your own hands, woman! Now see what you have done?" Even though he tried to sound angry, he failed. Pride and pleasure filled him at the bravery shown by this woman who had somehow entrapped his heart and body. When she had quieted enough to speak, it took great gulps of air for her to manage it.

"You would have stopped. I couldn't let you," she finally managed to say, still sobbing. "I didn't realize it would hurt so much, but . . ."

"It wouldn't have, if you had let me finish." He watched

her face, willing Laydya to finally look at him. "There is always pain the first time, but not anymore. I give you my promise."

"How would you know, warrior? Have you taken many virgins?" Laydya hit his shoulder with all of her strength, which wasn't much. He only laughed, pulling her close.

"It is the nature of things," he answered, very pleased with himself. Gavilan flinched when she hit him again. He pulled away from her and saw her flinch from the pain, and was immediately concerned.

"Come . . . I have something to show you, and besides, the water will ease the pain." He slipped from her body and stood, unashamed of standing there completely naked as the day he was born. He held his hand down to pull her up, a mischievous grin on that handsome face waiting for her to take his hand.

Laydya could just glimpse a shadow of the boy who had come here long ago to escape the gossip of the Keep or the burdens that had plagued him. Gone were the lines of anger and hurt that had been there just hours ago. Also gone for now were the sensations of loneliness she had been sensing from since they had arrived at Dragonslair. He stood in all his glory as just a man who wanted to show her his favorite place.

Chapter 11

Gavilan moved to the edge of the small lake and drove into the clear waters. He surfaced some distance away, and motioned for her to follow.

Laydya had learned to swim when she was very young, but it had been in the river near her home, which was never very clear. Diving into warm crystal clear waters that caressed her naked skin she was captivated by how wonderful it felt. When she swam close to Gavilan, he grinned, then dove beneath the surface, leaving her paddling on the surface alone.

She waited several minutes, waiting for him to resurface, and when he didn't Laydya began to panic. No one could hold their breath that long, she was sure of it! Diving down, she searched the clear waters for him, but couldn't find him anywhere. Over and over she drove, until her breath was coming in gasps, but still there was no sign of Gavilan. She was really starting to panic when something touched her leg, and she felt the warm hand move up to the flat of her belly, and then her breast. Lips tenderly took the nipple in his mouth, causing Laydya to forget all about her panic. When his head came up for air, Laydya nearly dunked him again.

"You scared me to death!" she yelled, pushing him away from her. "Don't tell me you can swim like a fish, because I will not believe it!"

"Come," he whispered, pulling her back against him with ease. "I'll show you my special place." With those profound words, he dove again, this time waiting for her just beneath the surface.

As she followed, Laydya was at first terrified that he led them to their deaths. Down he dove, leading her toward a break in the rocks just below the surface. As she watched, he disappeared between the cracks. When she maneuvered her way between them, a light above her head drew her upward. To Laydya's delight she found Gavilan sitting on a ledge in a cave. The air was humid and thick with age, but otherwise it was dry and up away from the edge of the pool. When he helped her out of the water, she could see several objects behind him.

"This is where you disappeared to when you didn't want to be found, isn't it?" she gasped, wiping water from her face.

There was an old wooden box with candles and flint lying nearby. A bedroll, some books covered with cobwebs, all were reminders of a small boy who felt he had to disappear for a while in order to survive in his small world. Laydya shivered as she gazed at the closeness of the cave walls. Gavilan saw it, took in the paleness of her complexion, and decided it was time to get back to the surface.

"Let's get back, shall we? I can see you don't deal well with tight places such as caves." He grinned at her shocked expression, then worried as she shook her head.

"It's not the caves, Gavilan. It is something more, a feeling I have that there may be danger ahead. Do not ask me to explain. I can't put words what some of these feelings are when they come, it's just that a sense of foreboding tells me that we will encounter something like this soon," she added when she saw he was about to say more.

"Well, let's get going. I think I have a way of making you forget these feelings." He pulled her into the water, and soon they were back in the sunlight of the grotto.

Gavilan did make her forget about the dangers they faced. They had spent the rest of the afternoon learning each other's bodies and how to make each other crazy. It didn't take much, Laydya had to smile to herself. That man could make a saint forget their name, Laydya decided, as they rode back toward the keep at dusk.

Both rode in silence, relishing the new closeness they felt in each other. She wondered if fate had taken a hand in this match, but resolved not to question it too closely. It was too fragile and new to tear apart and examine. Laydya just wanted to bask in the aftermath of Gavilan's lovemaking for as long as it lasted.

As the two of them neared the keep's outer walls, neither were surprised to see Eric leaning against the stone walls with a dark shaped panther at his feet. Both of them laughed outrageously as Damen reached up and took a playful swat at Eric's robes, and the swearing that reached their ears was colorful to say the least!

All through the next week, Laydya was sure this was what paradise was like as she and Gavilan explored their new closeness that seem to have no bounds. By day Gavilan worked from dawn to dusk inspecting the fortifications of Dragonslair or supervised the men on the training field, while she and Eric searched the ancient scrolls for any possible crack in Kasadim's scheme to overtake the land. It was only after the evening meal and everyone found their own beds that Gavilan would come silently to her chamber, and the world outside would disappear as he showed her the wondrous delights that awaited them. During these quiet times, lying temporarily sated and exhausted in his strong arms Laydya would let herself think upon the reasons *why* Gavilan felt it was necessary to come unnoticed to her chambers. Everyone in the keep knew what they were doing behind those huge closed doors, yet the pretense of hiding it grated on her nerves, causing apprehension and uncertainty to cloud the very reasons why she had come to Dragonslair in the first place. Their time was too short as far as she was concerned. She could feel darkness coming.

At night, after Gavilan wrapped her in his arms, Laydya's dreams were filled with shadows and memories of Lowen's iridescent cocoon locking her friend in perpetual silence. In the background all she could hear was the evil laugh of a madman. She would search the ether of her dreams, sword in hand ready to fight only to wake screaming and drenched in sweat as she shook within Gavilan's strong arms. The longer they waited the worse the dreams became.

Thinking sleeping in Gavilan's quarters might help, she had broached the subject of meeting him in his quarters after last meal. Their first argument after becoming lovers had been loud and heated.

"I'll meet you in your chambers, Laydya. Tis best so just wait for me." Gavilan had started to walk away and she had pulled him around, standing in front of him just as she would do any other man who she felt was her equal.

"You're ashamed of me!" she whispered, eyes moist at the thought after all they had shared. Laydya had turned and started to stalk away but her temper had gotten the test of her.

"Well, think on this," she turned back, shouting for all to hear. "I have claimed you, Gavilan of Dragonslair. You can run. You can deny it, but you will not hide from me."

The hall had been full and every head turned as the two of them stared at each other, Laydya's temper high, head proud. She was too angry to see the proud tilt of Gavilan's head as he watched her or she would have been mortified to realize he wasn't angry at her. In fact, he was so proud of her at that moment he could barely keep his mouth shut.

"Malady, I have been trying to save your honor," he responded, tone reverent and just as loud.

"Be damn with my honor. You should know by now what everyone thinks of me and I don't give a fig what others think at this point. But you will be in my bed tonight or I will come looking for you, do you understand me?" Her smug shout echoed in the hall as she stalked from the room as great laughter rang from the men left at the tables. Her face was flaming as she slammed into her rooms and covered her face with her hands.

Never had she humiliated herself like that before but there was no way Laydya could allow him to push her away or treat her like some serving wrench. She would stand tall and accept the challenges before her and he could stand by her side or not. If Gavilan would not move her into his quarters and was ashamed of her refusing to stay with her past dawn, then so be it. She would accept his arms when she went to sleep and pray he would someday be there when she woke.

Dougal was finally healing although his temperament left much to be desired. Laydya would come upon him as he looked east out of a door or window and the look in his grey eyes tore at her heart. She dare not broach the subject concerning Lowen though, having made that mistake only once and had vowed not to again. Not until she could offer her friend answers to his questions!

Answers! Were there any?

Laydya asked herself that on this night as she lay snuggled against Gavilan's hard body while the cool night breeze flowed through the windows to cool the sweat on their bodies. He had tried to tire her out in hopes her mind would be too tired and the dreams would stay away but she knew that wouldn't be the case. They were telling her something, were clues to what was to come if she could just figure out what. Just like the dreams before her home had been invaded these where clues Laydya had to figure out before it was too late.

Could Kasadim be defeated? Could she and Gavilan really reverse the destruction and horror that lay upon the land because of a madman?

The deep night was gloriously soft as Gavilan lay holding her close, her body exhausted from his many assaults to not only her body but her emotions. Sweat glistened off their bodies illuminated by the candle light flickering off her bedroom walls and Laydya only wished her dark nightmares were as mellow.

"Gavilan, we've got to leave soon! We have to go to the Mountain of the Kings," she whispered as she lay resting across his chest. When he didn't make a sound, she gently punched him in the side.

"Did you hear me?" Another jab and his grunt insured her that she finally had his attention. Like lightning, she found herself pulled completely on top of him with their faces nose to nose.

"Are you sure about this? There is no doubt, no possible way Lowen could have misconstrued what it would take to get to Kasadim?" Gavilan stroked her naked shoulder as he spoke, unaware that he did so.

"None!!" Laydya's ardent reply was quick and firm. She could sense his concern as it rippled through her mind, dread choking her as it had so often of late. "You still don't trust in this, do you?"

His deep sigh gave nothing away but she refused to give on this. She had to complete her mission in order to release Lowen from her self-induced prison. Finishing this was the only way any of them would ever be safe again. Laydya had promised herself she would not use her gifts to *read* Gavilan but it monstrously hard not to when this stubborn warrior shut her out. Gavilan had to trust in this on his own. Anything else and it would not only be unfair, it would only lead to their destruction!

"I've sensed your restlessness lately and knew you would want to continue on this dangerous quest soon. Can you blame me for doubting, for wanting to keep you safe?" he finally said, looking at her.

Strong arms pulled her closer, the scent of him storming over defenses and hacking down the invisible barrier of hurt that Laydya hadn't known was going up until this instant. Laydya tried to smiled, knowing how much it cost him to admit the smallest amount of give in this blooming relationship.

"We have to have faith in each other, Gavilan. That is our strength, each other!" She sealed her vow with a kiss.

Gavilan felt the kiss all the way to his bones.

This woman who had such innate gifts and who was still so innocent actually chose to belonged to him and it boggled his mind. Once he could breathe again, he found himself staring into eyes the same color as Damen's which was so unusual. He saw determination and passion, love and devotion and need. A deep, driving need.

"Fine, then we tell Dougal on the morrow, and leave at first light the following dawn. But you have got to promise me one thing, woman!" He watched that impish smile that was so distracting turn up the corners of her mouth and groaned. How could he ever have thought he could resist this woman for any length of time. "Promise me if danger approaches, and you feel it, you will tell me immediately. No trying to protect me. We are in this together, and we use what skills both of us possess to stay alive."

"Aye, my mighty warrior. You have my promise, and much, much more!!"

Chapter 12

Come morning found both Laydya and Gavilan eager to leave the keep without a backward glance. Dougal was furious, Lord Invor was shouting, and Eric was grinning like a fool. Gavilan's two stepsisters, Dena and Alexis were sitting near the fireplace on the far side of the great hall as far away as possible trying not to eavesdrop on the arguments but still keep track of what was going on. They didn't want to miss a single tidbit of this so that all of the gossip would be fresh once the smoke cleared. However, no one could miss it, unless they were truly deaf. The uproar was so loud even Damen had decided to hide in Laydya' room.

Laydya stood with her long legs slightly apart and remained quiet next to Gavilan. She unconsciously had her right hand resting on the sword at her him, watching as Lord Invor recounted for the hundredth time why the two of them shouldn't leave the castle without an entire battalion of warriors. She was so proud of Gavilan as he stood patiently listening, a faraway look on his face. She was struck with a fierce protectiveness as she watched Gavilan stand there so tall and imposing in a royal blue shirt and black leather breeches clinging to every muscle in those thick, muscled thighs. Laydya couldn't help feel the rush of yearning for the quiet of her chambers they had left only an hour ago so they could continue where they had left off.

As she watched her lover, Laydya was sure his manner in dealing with his father was an ingrained habit gained from his youth before being sent away to foster at another Keep. Doubtlessly he didn't win many arguments with the imposing man pacing back and forth in front of them. What she couldn't figure out was why Eric was looking so happy. The odd tingling that always left her breathless stirred the nap of her neck. Startled she glanced at Eric, and found his eyes drilling into hers. She felt rather than heard his answers.

"Yes, you will both go, but so will I. Not so much in body, for I am of more use to you here than out on the road. I have been researching the scrolls and must continue in order to help you with this quest if both of you are to survive. Now you know how to contact me, Lady Laydya, so do not forget." He then returned his attention back to his father.

" . . . and another thing! Just what makes you so sure she is the one spoken of in the prophecies? How can you be so blind to be led around by a mere slip of a girl by your cock?" Lord Invor turned his anger toward Laydya for the first time, and in that instant she knew where Gavilan came by his nature.

"You will not speak of her in that tone!" Gavilan's low growl echoed among the high ceilings as if he had shouted it, silencing everyone in the room.

"You dare tell me how to act in my own home? Someone who may even be a threat to it?" Lord Invor got right up in Gavilan's face, daring him to say more.

"She will be treated with the same respect as any high born Lady. She is the granddaughter of Falconwood, heir of Valeyrian." As he counted off her numerous titles, an ache formed in Laydya's chest. There was so much at stake if they failed and this stubborn man was so afraid of losing his son he couldn't see the danger to his own lands. They were so much alike they see it, so blinded by the past that neither of them could see the other's strength.

"And just what are you staring at, miss? Have I suddenly grown two heads and a thorny tail?" She hadn't realized her thoughts had wondered until Lord Invor was almost nose to nose with her, his flushed face inches away even as he towered over her.

She didn't flinch a muscle as her screamed in her face but felt Gavilan start to move in to protect her when she gently put her hand on his arm.

"Your father doesn't frighten me, Gavilan. I finally see what you will look like in your later years if I don't watch you very closely," she said with a grin.

"Why you . . ." Lord Invor roared and turned to stand near the fireplace. He didn't seem to notice the mantel had been repaired from Gavilan's earlier temper fit. He didn't hear the mumbling going on from where his daughters sat across the hall in total shock at this small slip of a woman was actually standing up to their father. Not even their dead mother had done such a thing, and she had been known throughout to kingdom for her own fits of rage. All Lord Invor heard was the ringing in his ears were her words. Gavilan would be like him when he grew older.

Gavilan....the pain was unbearable. What had he done? Dear God, what had he done?

When he turned back to face the small group, there was the slightest trace of moisture in his eyes. He looked at his oldest son, truly so like himself, and felt the pain again. It must have been mirrored in his eyes, for suddenly Gavilan was next to him, not really embracing him, but his arm came around his shoulders none the less.

Laydya quickly shooed the sisters up the stairs as Eric led a still complaining Dougal toward the kitchens. Laydya followed them, glancing over her shoulder once with a soft smile. Gavilan and his father needed some time to themselves to sit in the huge winged backed chairs. Hopefully, talking to each other rather than yelling *at* each other they could finally forge a bond that was too long in coming.

She encountered a servant in route to the kitchens, and ask that wine be taken to the two men to the young girl not to interrupt them. She watched from the distance and saw Gavilan glance up as he took his goblet. Their eyes met for just a moment, but in that second Laydya saw his gratitude in his green depths. Smiling, she entered the kitchens.

"Now wait just a minute, Eric! She cannot go running all over the country side with that big ox, not without protection. It is just not right man, she is still a lady!" Dougal was in his own rage as Laydya came to stand next to him.

"I will have you know, Dougal, that Gavilan is quite capable of protecting me. And besides, you are not well enough for this journey yet. Damen will be with us so you need to allow me to do what you and Lowen have trained me to do." Even sitting next to him he towered over her, trying to bend her will to his.

"You cannot go alone! You must take someone with you to protect your . . . ah . . ." Dougal seem to run out of words suddenly.

"Yesss . . . ?" Laydya drew out so innocently, looking down at the table and trying to keep the deep blush from coloring her face

"Damnit girl, you know exactly what I mean, stop acting like you don't!" Dougal took a long swallow of ale, looking down at her.

"Dougal," she whispered.   "'Tis all right, I love him."
"But . ."

"Cease, please!. 'Tis meant to be, can you not see that? Lowen knew it, and so do you! I know it's hard for you to stop worrying about me. But it's best if you stay here   just help Lord Invor and Eric protect their home. I can take care of myself, thanks to you." Laydya was instantly contrite at mentioning the Druidess, for Dougal's eyes clouded to a stormy grey.

"I have to do this, Dougal. It's the only way to free her, to free all of us. If we don't succeed this madman will leech the life from everything and everyone I hold dear. You've seen what he does to innocents and now it is time for me to fulfill my destiny! Don't make it harder for me than it already is," she pleaded, refusing to give in to his stronger will. As she bent up to gently kiss his cheek, the huge warrior turned bright red.

"I'm not going to be able to talk you out of this one, am I?" Seeing the shake her head, Dougal let out a long sigh. "Your grandfather would kill me himself if anything happens to you. You know that, don't you?"

"No, he would not! He would praise you for such a good job of raising me." Tears pooled and slipped down her face and making her eyes reflect the lights of the kitchen. Dougal pulled her to him and held her close, his strong arms gently rocking her.

"Take care of that big ox in there. He got himself caught once before, and he just might do it again." Dougal laughed at the look Laydya gave him, while Eric managed to keep his amusement contained to a quiet rumble.

"We will be fine." Laydya told both them, silently crossing her fingers.

"Since you are bent on doing this, I will be leaving for the Circle of Stones as soon as I can ride. Eric assures me that my arm will be almost as good as new in a week and I want to be there when you obtain Lowen's release." The big warrior refused to look directly at her, and Laydya contained her smile. "Besides, when the witch is herself again there is something I wish to ask her. We will meet you back at Valeyrian once your journey is finished!"

Dougal pulled her into another bear hug and hurriedly left the kitchens by the back exit. Laydya watched him go, praying he was right, and that she would see both of her friends again!

"Now tell me all about Gavilan's past and this trouble with his father. We don't have much time since Gavilan wants to leave at first light. I want you to come to my chambers while I get ready." Laydya was stalking up the back stairs before she realized Eric wasn't behind her. She turned to see him still sitting by the large table, a goblet held in mid-air.

"Are you just going to sit there? I don't want Gavilan and his father interrupted, so they can talk out this thing between them. You best just come along so you stay out of mischief."

Laydya started up the stairs again, pleased to hear Eric's soft footfalls behind her. Her mind was still whirling. Gavilan and his father were finally talking, Would that mean he would become the appointed heir again? She refused to worry about it for now praying that their future would together. They had too many obstacles ahead of them to be worrying over that at the moment. Pushing the sudden ache away from her heart, Laydya decided she would store away as many memories of their time together as possible. She would never ask Gavilan to forsake his birthright, just as she could not walk away from hers. Laydya tried to smile, sending up a silent prayer that they both would be in one piece when this was over, so they could fight about the future!

Chapter 13

As Gavilan led the way out of Dragonslair couldn't stop from looking back one last time. Dougal stood next to Eric at the arched gates with his elbow braced on the shorter man's shoulder for support. She was even more surprised when Lord Invor moved from the shadows to stand next to his youngest son with a solemn frown on his face and looking very much the lord of the castle. She couldn't stop herself from wondering if this might be the last time if she saw Dougal again. Would all return to normal when and if their journey was successful.

Giving herself a mental shake of her head Laydya turned back around and locked onto Gavilan's wide shoulders, watching for Damen out of the corner of her eye. The countryside around Dragonslair was dotted with farmsteads and homes until they reached an area both of them had discussed at length and argued about even more. It was almost uninhabitable by most and Dougal had been adamant that they be on their guard no matter what. Few had ventured into these lands and returned to tell about it.

The became extremely rough once they reached the badlands, and Laydya repeatedly thanked the stars above that Dougal wasn't along. The horses had a hard time over the rocky terrain and at times they were forced to lead their mounts over barely passable ground. Deep rocky gullies lay at the bottom of most of the trails streams rushing down the steep ravines in white foamed splendor. As they navigated barely passible areas, steep slopes were covered with brush, tall trees and wild flowers. The thick stands of timber made the going slow, and Laydya felt thorns prick her even through the sturdy leather leggings and thick vest Gavilan had insisted she wear. Crossing one particularly large stream toward the end of the second day almost unseated Laydya something rarely done since she had first started riding. After safely getting to the other side, Gavilan called finally called a halt.

He had been silent for the most part since leaving the castle, barely talking unless it was about the smallest things such as making camp. Laydya hadn't tried to push the issue. Being raised around warriors and she recognized when a man needed time to sort out things before talking about them. She had no doubt Gavilan would eventually talk to her, but she hoped it would be soon since he hadn't touched since they had left the Keep.

A slow heat permeated her being, awakening the fierce need for Gavilan. It was the same one Laydya had come to associate with his very passion and she felt a deep sense of loss from not having his touch in so long. Since their last night together she had burned with such a need for this fierce warrior that bordered on obsessive and it terrified her!

Their first night after leaving the Keep when he had simply pulled her close and told her to go to sleep, Laydya was a little concerned but figured it was due to so much having transpired in the last couple of days. The fight with his father, the upcoming journey, all of it was weighing heavy on her mind so it was no wonder it could be bothering Gavilan.

However, he just pulled her against his chest and held her. No kiss, nothing!

When the following night was a repeat, she just lay there long after she heard his even breathing, a sure sign he was asleep. Something was bothering Gavilan, but Laydya made herself wait. Even Damen sensed it because he curled close to her front as if blanketing her between the two of them.

Gavilan needs time, she kept telling herself. Whatever was bothering him would eventually work itself out.

On the third day of the miserable terrain and an uncommunicative warrior, almost being nearly unseated from her horse and drenched to the skin, Laydya's temper was just barely under control. Gavilan found a suitable place and they made camp, but he left just as quickly and disappeared into the forest without a word while Laydya pulled her only other set of dry clothes from her pack.

"Stupid oaf, who does he think he is anyway," Laydya mumbled under her breath as she looked for a place to clean up and change. Damen simply sat watching as she raged at the empty glen. "Barely says a word in two days, then orders camp early."

When Laydya had changed into the dry clothes, she stomped back toward the clearing where Gavilan had tied the horses. As she looked around, Laydya could hear the forest creatures getting ready for night, the shuffling of the horses, but nothing else.   All was stillness, and there wasn't a sign of Gavilan anywhere!

"I guess 'tis my turn to fix a meal!" she called loudly to Gavilan, but received no answer. "Well, let's see how he likes my cooking!" she mumbled as Damen curled nearby cleaning his ebony coat as if he hadn't a care in the world.

Laydya held no claim to being able to cook. In fact, about all she could do was put out some hard cheese, bread and ale. Again she wondered just what Gavilan would say when he found out there were a lot of domestic chores she couldn't do, like sewing and mending. What would happen when he realized he was getting a woman trained in a man's world, not in a woman's?

"Are you brooding, or trying to burn a hole in the cheese?" Laydya jumped and had her dagger drawn before she realized it. Gavilan stood leaning against a tree not more than three feet from her.

How did he move around so quietly without her hearing him? she fumed silently!

"Where were you? You scared me to death!" Laydya shouted, instantly contrite. The look on Gavilan's face was priceless.

"Why are you so mad?" Hearing his soft question after so many days of being ignored ignited the short fuse she had on her temper. To top it off, Damen lopped over to curl a long black tail around Gavilan's leg and leaning against the warrior's side while shamelessly begging for a scratch. Laydya refused to beg for his touch, or anything else.

"You mean you finally decided to speak to me?" Laydya swung back around to the fire, poking a stick into the embers. She never heard him move, but suddenly Gavilan held her in his strong arms.

"Poor Princess, I have really been a bear lately, huh?." He tried to kiss her, but Laydya turned her head, thus he kissed the hollow just below an ear.

"I am sorry, kitten. I have been battling myself trying to figure out what to do about you!" His whispered apology stung her soul.

She caught his face in both of her hands, looking deep into the forest depths of his eyes to see his torment so like her own. Laydya knew her lover had many changes that must be bombarding him and it hurt her very soul that she only added to those. Gavilan was a man of worth who believed in honor and courage. What they would be fighting went against everything he believed in.

"Oh Gavilan, you had me so scared. I thought . . ." she stopped, her chin trembling in an attempt to not allow the tears she had fought for so long to fall. If they ever started Laydya was afraid they might never stop.

"You thought I had my fill of you?" His eyes never left her face and she could only nod. She couldn't get a single word past the tightness in her throat. "Ah love, how could you doubt me after all I tried to teach you in that quiet bedchamber? I just had to work out some things in my own mind before I could touch you again. You have the strangest way of making me forget the past, present and the future!"

Gavilan sat down on a large rock next to the fire and reached for Laydya, pulling her onto his lap. He cuddled her tight against his chest and wrapped his strong arms around her.

"Did Eric tell you of what happened with my father?" he whispered.

"As much as he knew. I told him I would wait for you to tell me the rest." She felt him take a deep breath and Laydya wondered what was to come.

"My father has proclaimed me heir, much to Eric's joy. Eric never wanted it, never felt he could carry the burdens of his calling and that of a kingdom as well." He paused with a long sigh. "I don't want the responsibility of Dragonslair, not on my father's terms, yet I cannot walk away from them either."

"Shhh," she whispered, kissing his forehead. "Somehow we'll work it all out when this is finished, Gavilan. Somehow, we will find a way."

Laydya ran her fingertips across his strong chin, up his chiseled cheek bones to the lock of black hair that always fell over his forehead and out of place. Laydya watched his eyes turn dark as the fire jumped between them. She kissed his chin, then each eye, finally to settle on the mouth that brought her so much joy. Wanton, that was what she had become! Laydya could feel his heartbeat against her breasts as she deepened the kiss. Gavilan's arms tightened around her as she continued her assault to make him forget the woes they faced and just be in the moment, to feel what was between them.

Gavilan was determined to be gentle. Lately their coming together had been a fierce, needy coupling rocking both of them and sending them into exhausted sleep. Neither of them noticed as Damen disappeared into the approaching darkness to hunt.

Like dry timber licked by hungry flames, Gavilan felt the fire in his blood burn and knew this woman in his arms was the only one who would ever be able to do this to him again. He slowly caressed her hips, trailing his hand to her waist and up to her firm breasts, forcing himself to go slow. Everywhere he touched the flames grew higher. Before long, the woman in his arms was moaning his name, her body begging for the release only he could give her. In moments, he had their clothes laying in a pile next to the fur throws that made up their bed.

Gavilan trailed kisses across her shoulders and down her stomach, causing nerve endings to pulse like quicksilver fire. He paid homage to each twin peak of her breasts, while his calloused hands slid down her stomach to tickle her naval. His mouth followed their trail, sending her higher still to the peak of pleasure. As his hand found the valley of her thighs, Laydya instinctively spread them to allow him access. His magic fingers found the treasure, gently pushing her closer to the beckoning brightness.

Gavilan's tongue laved soft skin down her stomach, over one hip to finally find the valley of soft curls. At the first touch of his sensual lips, Laydya tried to pull away but he held her still.

"Let me love you here, too. Let me show you!" Laydya barely heard his hoarse plea, so lost in the wondrous sensations coursing through her.

As Gavilan continued to lovingly taste her, lapping the essence from her folds as he held her beneath him and enjoyed every sound she made. He wanted to hear her pleasure, feel it around his fingers and he pushed deep into her moist channel and taste the very magic that was Laydya.

"Let go, kitten, let it come," he whispered, lifting his head to look up her long body.

On and on he pushed her, until he was sure Laydya would shatter. When he knew he couldn't hold on a moment more, he moved up to cover her and took those full lips, sheathing his manhood in one swift thrust.

Gavilan was striving hard for control. He wanted her to find release first, but as he pushed deep within her, Laydya tightened around him, stroking with tightening velvet softness. Unable to withstand her gentle torture, Gavilan lost control. With a lover's gentleness he took her with him, moving to the ancient rhythm of lovers.

"Please . . ." she cried. "Gavilan!" was all she could scream as he pushed deeper, taking her with him.

Laydya cried out as he began to move, deep long strokes that sent her reeling over the edge. They spiraled together, reaching for the brightness of that was just out of reach. She screamed, reaching for paradise and dragging Gavilan with her.

Her breathing was finally back to normal when she realized Gavilan had rolled them onto their sides. They were covered with fur throws against the evening chill, his warmth a welcome security after so much that had happened. From his breathing she knew he wasn't asleep, but when she leaned up to look at him, she was surprised to see him staring at her with such an odd look.

"Did I not please you?" She knew she had, and her look told him so.

"Nay woman, you did not please me!" His denial caught her off guard for just a second, until she saw he was trying very hard to hide a very satisfied grin. She landed an elbow in his ribs, trying to turn her back to him, but he didn't allow her to get that far. With amazing quickness he had her laying on top of him, hardly ruffling the furs.

"Woman, you know you please me well enough! Why must you fight me?" His outright grin was so devastating, Laydya felt its heat burn her.

"Sometimes Gavilan, a woman wants to hear the words!" she said so softly he almost didn't hear her.

"Ah, she looks for compliments now. A true woman's trait."

"I do not . . . it is just . . ." How could she tell him she didn't know of woman's things? The despair which crept into her eyes was Gavilan's undoing.

"What is it, Laydya?"

The tears Laydya had fought back for so long rushed forward. Before she could stop them, they were spilling down her face and mingling with the still drying sheen of perspiration on both of them. Saints above, she had never cried more than a few times in all the years, before meeting this man!

Gavilan didn't know what to make of it. One minute she was teasing him like a wanton sex kitten and the next crying like a babe. He could only hold her, and wait until she quieted. When he heard the sobs turn to hiccups, Gavilan lay her next to him, propping up on an elbow.

"Ok, are re you going to tell me why the tears, or do I have to guess?" He was trying to make her smile again, but she looked away from him toward the fire.

"Well . . ." he asked again when she refused to look at him.

"You know so little about me, Gavilan. What will you do when you realize I am not like other women you have known?" She sounded so pitiful, Gavilan became worried.

"How are you different? Do you have some secret which has escaped me?" He picked up a lock of her hair, playing with it as he waited for her to tell him what was wrong. He wasn't going to allow her to go to sleep until she finally opened up as to what had been eating at her for so long.

"I don't think you will like me much once you know my true short comings!" Laydya wouldn't look at him. She didn't want to see the rejection in his eyes when he learned she couldn't do things like running a household that most young women were taught from the time they could walk. Laydya knew his patience was getting short when he let out a long sigh.

"What things can you do, and not do, that will make me think ill of you? Out with it now or we will be here all night and never get to sleep." She forced herself to look just over his shoulder.

"I cannot cook, or sew. I know absolutely nothing but the basics of healing, at least not until recently! I can run a household fairly well, because I can tally the storerooms better than most, which keeps servants honest. But as to other, more gentile practices of women, I know very little."

She squeezed her eyes shut, waiting for the rebuke she was sure would come. When all was quiet, she chanced a look from lowered lids.

Gavilan was smiling. The big oaf was actually grinning from ear to ear, and very pleased with himself for some reason she couldn't fathom.

"You are not surprised, are you?" Laydya finally said in awe.

"Do you not think Dougal has tried to fill me in on all your faults as to what he calls women's' training?" At her gasp, he chuckled. "You can't blame him, Laydya. He was just trying to test my mettle. I have known for some time that you lack training in some areas." Gavilan softened his admission with a sweet, lingering kiss that curled her toes.

"And you do not mind? I mean . . . it doesn't make a difference to you?"

"None!" His smile broadened, if it were possible. "You see my little warrior, once this quest is finished, and you have the time to learn other things, I have full confidence that you will learn whatever it is you set your mind to." Gavilan pulled her close for another searing kiss. "But until then, it will be my pleasure to teach you all I know in the areas you are such an apt pupil." It was a long time before either of them fell into an exhausted sleep.

Chapter 14

The moon was high overhead when Laydya woke with a feeling that something wasn't off. She felt Gavilan's even breathing as he held her tight to his chest. She could feel his heartbeat under the palm of her hand where she rested it over his thick wrist. Concentrating on the sounds around her, Laydya tried to figure out what had pulled her from such a sound sleep.

Crickets sang softly around them, the screech of an owl catching its prey echoed off in the distance. Both horses were restless, but not frightened at whatever it was that had seemed out of place. Damen's deep rumble as he slept next to Gavilan assured her that nothing approached that could harm them.

Surprisingly, she had the oddest need to pull the globe that Eric had given her and hold it. The more she tried to push the thought away, the stronger it became. With slow, careful movements, Laydya untangled herself from Gavilan's warm embrace, pulling a fur wrap around her near nakedness to ward off the chill of the night.

Sitting near the fire, but not very far from Gavilan, she pulled the blood red orb from its protective pouch. As soon as she smoothed a hand over it, it began throbbing with a life of its own. She had refused to take it out of the pouch since they had left the Circle of Stones, unable to hold the last gift Lowen had bestowed on her. Now she felt the power it radiated, and thoughts of the Druidess flooded her with loneliness, and strength!

The sensations flowed through her, undulating with each pulse of crimson light, which wasn't heat but still warmed her from within. A haze began to surround Laydya as she held the globe, the darkness around surrounding her field of vision retreating in eerie stages as if pushed away by some unknown force. She could still see Gavilan asleep under the furs, and hear the horses moving about near the trees but it all seemed as if through a veil of some sort. Damen instantly appeared next to her as if from nowhere, and the haze gave it all a dreamy quality.

Concentrating on the light, Laydya felt its warmth draw her deeper, until she thought she heard Eric's voice somewhere in the distance. Startled, she looked around her, thinking he had changed his mind and followed them after all but as soon as she took her eyes away from the globe, she lost his voice. Confused, she concentrated harder on the red light, and clearly heard Eric's voice again.

"Yes, it is I. Did I not tell you I would be along on your journey?"

Laydya heard the voice in her mind, not her ears. How strange? How did Eric know she had the globe.

"Don't worry about that right now, just listen! My strength is fading fast, for I have only practiced this once before."

"Is all well with Dragonslair? Is something wrong with Dougal?" Laydya couldn't believe she was actually holding a conversation with Eric through the globe. This unconventional means of communicating would take some getting used to.

"All is well here, but I have discovered something I thought you needed to know. Something that affects you, Laydya!"

"What do you mean?" Silently her eyes probed at the globe. Could Eric have uncovered a shortcut to this riddle? Was there another way to get to Kasadim?

"No, there is no other way!" She forgot that she was sending her own thoughts as well. This means of communication could be tricky if one didn't watch it, and now she understood Lowen's warnings while trying to teach her so quickly.

"I found some old scrolls in the archives of the Order. It lays mention to the fact that the chosen one is related by blood, although ancient, to the Evil one. You must take care, Lady Laydya. If he should try to use this against you, you need to be warned." Eric's thoughts drummed into her brain as at their mean. Related by ancient blood?   But how?

"From your mother's side, I expect. I questioned Dougal about it, and it seems that her clan name was the same as Kasadim's before he took his present, or should I say unholy, name."

"But how could that be? Is that why the quest is on my shoulders, because of blood?"

"Yes, and he could very well think you would not know about it. Something you evidently do not know about your mother's people, is that at one point in time, several generations before she was born, one of her forefathers' angered a supreme mage of a dark and evil order who was, unfortunately, a brother. If it had not been for a nurse who hid a girl-child from the assassins, the bloodline would have been wiped out.

"Kasadim must be a direct decedent from that wizard! From all I can find out about his early experiments, he was looking for the way to eternal life and power. But he could not gain the gifts you have, no matter how he tried. He did some hideous things, Lady Laydya. Things that even this many years later were barbaric in his search for the gifts you now have. I warn you, so you can be on your guard at all times."

"But we have not had an incident since leaving the stones. So far our journey has been totally without one assault."

"That is because he cannot leave Valeyrian lands. It seems the Order put a curse on him when they tried to do away with him the last time. They realized too late he could transform into smoke and escape, so they bound him to the land, which his feet last touched. Valeyrian Land!"

"You mean he was . . . killed . . . ?"

"Yes!" the silent voice echoed on the moonlight.

Laydya began to shake from an inner chill and felt Damen curl around her back, his hissing echoing her inner thoughts. What could all of this mean, why had she been chosen?   Why?

"You cannot run from it, Lady Laydya! It is destiny that has determined your fate, your strength will have to be your victory." She felt the globe cool in her hands, its blood red light dimming to a dullness leaving her feeling cold and alone.

"Damen, what can this all mean?" Laydya whispered, clinging to the panther. The cat's warm tongue licked her wet face, bringing her back to the present.

Putting the globe away, Laydya sought the warm nest of their bed as she slid in next to Gavilan with Eric's words haunting her. She couldn't find sleep again until the eastern skies starting turning pink. Finally exhaustion claimed her, but not before she vowed to tell Gavilan everything.

Turning toward the man who was coming to mean more to her than life, she snuggled into his warm embrace. Strange he hadn't missed her, but her last thought was of the bond she knew they had which could carry her to do whatever she must.

Chapter 15

The Cavern of Tombs lay in a remote area of the mountains, made almost impassable due to deep ravines and gullies where the horses had a hard time finding sure footing. The ancient Kings of long ago were rumored to be buried here, entombed for all time away from grave diggers who held little reverence for the legends passed down through the ages. It was said that at one time all the kingdoms had been run by a great warrior, whose vassals were given each kingdom to safeguard from invaders.

Then the age of wizards came, causing terror and fighting among the vassals. No one knew where the magic-crafters came from. The only documents to survive the upheaval found said they appeared, worming their way into a close society of courts and the lives of the ruling classes. Empowered by rulers who feared them, a few of the sorcerers turned to the dark side of the arts, seeking to increase their knowledge in any way they found possible. Deaths could not be explained and people would disappear without cause. Terror and superstition caused the people of the land to turn against the upper class who supported the wizards as failed experiments became evident, especially when dead bodies were left along the road or near a village in plain sight for anyone to find as a reminder to keep their mouths shut and mind their own business. No one went out alone. Children were taught to fear the dark, their parents afraid they could be snatched away to be used in unspeakable experiments. When wars finally broke out, entire families were eliminated.

Out of the destruction emerged a mighty warrior named Ziocon, who enforced a new order where each lord claimed a kingdom, maintaining it with a force that were loyal only to that overlord. Each farmstead was expected to be self-sufficient by raising enough food to sustain the populace living within its borders and strong enough to protect its people. Thus, a feudal system was established.

When the Order of Shadows was uncovered, not all the sorcerers were found to be ruled by the dark side of power. Using the abilities of the ones sworn to their lords, the Order of Shadows was eventually vanquished by their own kind. The corrupted outcast wizards, who could change a normal sane man into frightening apparitions with experiments so hideous even their own kind could not stand them, were banished the only way they could be. Charms and runes were set against them so that they could never enter the kingdoms again, their spirits damned to roam the neither world.

Such a charm was placed on the Cavern of Tombs to keep anyone from entering to remove the remains of dead kings in revenge. All this Lowen had instilled Laydya during the trance transfer, but nothing had prepared her for the moment when she and Gavilan came to the entrance of the caverns they now sought.

No one would have been able to find it, not unless they understood an ancient riddle passed down from one Druid Priestess to the next, describing the path to the Tombs. Lowen had been emphatic that Laydya remember it. She had said the caverns were located in a hidden valley camouflaged by the surrounding landscape so that only at certain times of the day could one find the entrance. The way was marked, Lowen had said, but only to someone who knew what signs to look for, and followed them carefully. Otherwise, slow, agonizing death was a certainty.

The sister peaks stand stretching to the sky,
 The light of night is as bright as the dark of day.
Their thighs hold the secret of life,
 Beware the curse of the flay.

Laydya stood next to Gavilan as she repeated the riddle out loud, as much confused by it at the moment as Gavilan.

"What could Lowen mean? `Their thighs hold the secret'."

"I am not sure, Gavilan, but I think we should rest here tonight." Laydya whispered. There hadn't been any trouble since before going to Dragonslair, but the feeling of something about to happen continued to plague her senses since entering the valley where the Cavern of the Tombs was located.

Closing her eyes, Laydya let her inner sight roam free, tasting the fading threads of light for anything out of the ordinary. Nothing came back to her that would suggest evil lurked nearby, but still the knowledge that *something* wasn't right persisted.

She thought of the morning after Eric had contacted her through the globe, and Gavilan's reaction. He had been so furious at her for not waking him, it had actually been comical. But after Laydya had relayed all Eric had said, his anger had been replaced by caution.

Laydya was never out of his sight, never! If she needed privacy for her personal care, he would turn his back, but stayed within grabbing distance, as if he feared someone would reach out of a tree to pluck her away. The only concession he made was to let her share the watch at night as they neared their destination. Laydya had argued he would be of little use if he didn't sleep, and thankfully, he had seen the truth of it. They each took their turn, but the one sleeping always lay with their head in the other's lap. His need to have her close, protect her, was overwhelming and sent a sense of wonder to her core.

"What has you smiling, woman? Have you figured out the riddle?" Gavilan's question startled her out of her reverie, his frowning face looming over her like an avenging angel.

"No, I have not solved the riddle! But I have decided something else." Seeing her twinkling eyes, and mischievous grin Gavilan was instantly on guard.

"You are insatiable, wench!"

"Aye, but I don't think it has drained your strength, now has it?" Laydya announced over her shoulder as she began settling the horses for the night.

In short order they had a fire going with a succulent hare roasting over the pit. The sizzle of fat dropping into the fire was comforting as Laydya snuggled up against Gavilan who was propped up against a large tree. Damen lay nearby cleaning himself after hunting, his calmness a balm to Laydya's earlier apprehensions.

"I wonder what grandfather will think of you." Laydya let the question hang between them, waiting to see just what Gavilan would say.

"And just who might be this grandfather of yours be? You and Dougal have only mentioned him a handful of times, but each of you seem so filled with awe. Is he some paragon of virtue that lets his granddaughter grow up trying to be a man?" His words stung, igniting her temper.

Laydya swung around in his tight embrace to confront him but stilled at the look in his eyes. Those emerald orbs twinkled with merriment as he waited for the temper to flare, just has he had expected it to.

"You have taken to teasing very easily, my lord. Best you watch who you use it on, or they may act first and ask questions later!" she counseled, punching him in the stomach. He threw back his dark head, the laughter rumbling deep in his chest and escalating to fill the small glade where they camped.

"I have had a very good teacher, imp. Best you remember it in the future when you try to see what reaction you can get out of me." Gavilan tightened muscled arms around her.

Laydya chose to ignore him. Instead she shrugged out of his embrace, moving to test the hare since her stomach was growling and the smell was making it scream louder. Seeing it was done, she removed it from the spit and brought it over to Gavilan. With eating daggers they cut off bits and pieces, taking turns feeding each another. Soon they were finished and their thirst quenched with the fresh stream water. It was nice to settle against the tree and watch the flames dance in the fire, the sounds of night singing around them.

"So, are you going to tell me of this wonderful, doting relative, or do I have to wait to meet him?"

"His lands lay to the northwest of Valeyrian's. They were once part of ours long ago, but for some reason they were pensioned off to a distant ancestor of my mother's many, many generations ago. Aryon is most strict in his dealings with his people, yet fair and loyal to protect what is his. He will not take kindly to Valeyrian falling to attack by Kasadim."

Gavilan had grown very still while she talked, but she hadn't noticed until his continued silence caught her attention. When she turned, his eyes held a guarded look.

"Gavilan . . ."

"Are you talking about Argon, the Lord of Falconwood?" As she nodded, a gleam replaced the guarded look, Gavilan's expression so comical she could only stare. Seeing her speechless for the first time, he chuckled.

"We will not worry about your grandfather right now. I think all will be as it should be once all of this is over."

No matter how much Laydya tried to pry the reasons for his strange statements, Gavilan refused to say another word on the subject. It was at times like this that Laydya wished she could read other people's minds. It would help immensely in trying to figure out this warrior's strange smile as he built up the fire in readiness for sleep. Sometimes she thought she would never understand men!

Chapter 16

The entrance to the Caverns of the Kings looked exactly as Lowen had warned her! After carefully searching for any small signs placed in odd places on boulders around the entrance and taking several wrong turns they came upon the remains of other travelers who had found it unprofitable to search for the Caverns, Gavilan and Laydya finally stood before the entrance of the stone burial grounds. She and Gavilan could only stare at the gigantic entrance with its towering columns etched into the very fabric of the stone cliffs.

When they approached the huge stone doors only a giant could open, Laydya felt a shiver of foreboding shoot through her, leaving her weak and trembling. Damen began to pace and hiss, but otherwise he stayed close by her side. She reached deep for the calm Dougal had always taught her, finally signaling Damen to stay outside the Caverns. If anyone tried to approach them while inside, she didn't want to be caught off guard.

Gavilan didn't seem to notice her nervousness. All he could do was stare at the entrance and the odd diagram barely discernable on one of the columns.

Hidden in the crevice of rocks, the doors were carefully carved boulders that could be rolled away, if one knew the release mechanism that allowed it to move safely. Otherwise, Lowen had said there were a series of traps, which would stop anyone from entering. Neither of them could understand the runes at the top of the stone, but Laydya guessed it was the curse put there for the protection of those inside.

Repeating the riddle, Gavilan also noticed a V next to the stone. Above the symbol was the etching of a woman in long robes with the edge pulled up slightly, showing a foot resting on the top of each branch of the odd mark.

"Look at where she places her feet!" Gavilan whispered. Laydya moved closer to inspect the crude drawing.

"The sister peaks stand stretching to the sky." She gasped, then ran her hand over the drawing. "Gavilan, the V is the peaks stretching up!"

"Aye, but what does the gibberish about night and day?"

Laydya closely inspected the rest of the area around the strange drawing. Dust and deterioration had worn the surface down so that she could faintly see other drawings concealed beneath. Gently, she ran her hand over the others. Dust floated down the face of the stonewall, revealing the faint symbols more clearly. Just to the right of the V with the strange woman standing on top of it was a half-crescent moon. Laydya started to touch it, but Gavilan grabbed her hand.

"Better let me! We don't know what this is all about, just yet!" As Laydya stepped back, Gavilan placed one hand on the V and the other on the moon. As soon as both hands were flat, the huge stone next to them began to groan. Damen hissed at the motion, and Gavilan jumped back, moving his hands off the wall. As soon as he broke contact, the stone stopped.

Looking at each other, Laydya just shrugged her shoulders, unable to answer his silent question. Again Gavilan placed his hands in the same position. As the stone began to move this time, he kept still, awed by the gaping hole hidden behind stone. Laydya moved to stand next to him, looking over his shoulder, her mind boggled by the sheer size of cavity revealed. They could see very little from the entrance, but what she did see made Laydya's last dream all too real.

Leaving Damen to watch from the doorway, they cautiously proceeded inside, the huge proportions of the interior staggered the imagination. It was larger than any great hall either of them had seen, and the ceiling towered above them into darkness. A long isle ran down the middle of the cavern, a strange luminescent glow filtering down from somewhere above. On each side of the isle where the walls towered, every ten paces a stone indicated a tomb. Only the great kings were buried here, which was the highest form of honor that anyone could give a warrior. Laydya moved closer to Gavilan when she spied the dust covered stone throne sitting at the end of the aisle. All the way down each side were generations of kings, the throne a dark testimony to their reign while alive.

The ceiling of the cave somehow gave off light, a pale luminous glow that cast shadows in the corners, causing Laydya to shiver once again. Wherever, or however, the light was made, it was eerie and it made her skin crawl. Everything was exactly like her dream. The light, the throne sitting in a circle of light, the long aisle leading toward what . . .?

Pulling her sword from its sheath, Laydya ignored the sound of steel leaving leather as it echoed in the silence. Gavilan watched her, sensing her uneasiness at a dream made reality. It looked just as she had described it, except something was missing. Just as he took a step toward the throne, Laydya's hand came up to stop him. He turned around to see what was wrong when he noticed the movement in a dark corner of the cavern.

"Laydya . . . look out!"

Laydya's heart was in her throat as Gavilan shoved her behind him, her head buried in Gavilan's back. His sharp intake of breath at whatever he saw stiffened her spine and she stepped up beside him, sword ready. He had thrown her behind him just as a small creature moved into the light on noiseless feet. The creature was no taller than a four or five year old child, but its ancient face was one of nightmares, told to frighten children into submission. It's eyes glowed with an inner light much like the falcon Dougal had killed not long ago. The face was wrinkled so horridly, Laydya could hardly see where the nose ended and the mouth began. Long nails much like claws curved around fingertips, gleaming protrusions that could rip flesh in an instant. Laydya had no trouble imagining what they would do to unprotected flesh. The being came barely inside the light, standing there like a sentinel to guard their exit from this place of death. Laydya could feel Gavilan's arm tensed for battle if need be, but he didn't make a move toward the creature.

"Do, I know what you came for! But not shall you have it!" As the creature's strange singsong voice floated like a whisper in the silence, Damen's scream vibrated off the interior of the cavern, nearly deafening both of them. The being never indicated it even noticed.

Laydya looked over at Gavilan, wondering if he heard the same words, or was she the only one. She was relieved when Gavilan moved a slight step forward.

"If you know what we want, will you try to stop us?" Gavilan felt stupid talking to this creature, but as long as it made no threatening move toward them he would not harm it.

"Not life, can you have, if you take what you do want! *He* we must be served, or suffer!" The creature moved slightly forward, but Laydya and Gavilan raised their swords in warning and stepped back a pace.

"No can hurt something, not living like me. Death be here, so afraid I am not." It stepped forward again, and Laydya had the strangest feeling they were being herded toward something.

She felt a warning prickling on the waves of her senses, and instantly Damen's answering scream shook the dust from the ceiling and walls. A burning sensation throbbed at her side, and it took several moments to realize it was the blood red globe burning in the pocket of her tunic.

"Gavilan, it is a demon who has somehow gained entrance to the tombs without going through the door. `Tis Kasadim's message that he cannot be hurt, because he is already dead!"

"Impossible! How . . ."

"I don't know how, but I know!" she hissed. Gavilan to a chance to look at her face, saw the preoccupation in her eyes, and let out a curse.

"Do not speak his name! Not possible, what you wish. Master not send what you want for. Must not leave this place . . . place cannot leave. Death do you stalk, life you not have!" the creature whispered in its strange hypnotic song, and began swaying to and fro. The demon's claws began to glow as it raised one hand up to point it at Gavilan. Suddenly Laydya knew what would happen as the claws uncurled to point directly at Gavilan.

"Nooooo . . . Gavilan watch out!" Laydya tackled him broadside, bringing him down with a thud onto the hard dusty cavern floor just as a strange light flashed from the uncurled claws. She barely managed to get them out of the way.

"You *will not* take him from me, I will not exchange him for what I seek." Laydya was breathing hard from the fear of being certain she had almost lost Gavilan, and the dream becoming a reality.

She pulled the pouch holding the globe from her tunic pocket in one swift move. Holding it in her hand, Laydya concentrated on the creature as the bright light pulsed higher. With every beat of the light, the fiery heat radiated into her hand and up her arm. Holding the globe out toward the entity, Laydya felt the strength of the orb reach out on invisible strands of light to weave around the being.

The demon screamed, a demented sound of the damned that shattered eardrums and turned Laydya's blood to ice. Still she held the globe out, the red heat turning crimson, glowing and throbbing, changing the strange light of the cavern into its own soft red glow.

"Where is the shield?" she demanded of the demon, never taking her eyes from it. When it didn't answer, Laydya stepped closer, thrusting the glowing orb right into the creature's face. It couldn't seem to look away, but stood trembling with its strange eyes glued to the crimson glow.

"Where?" she yelled!

"Did you not tell me you saw it behind or beside the throne in your dream?" Gavilan's whisper came just over her shoulder. For the first time she remembered he stood next to her. At her nod, Gavilan slowly moved the few feet to the area near what looked like a throne. He tried to remember what Laydya had told him of her dream, but he didn't see anything round and tarnished, covered with dust and cobwebs.

Then from the shadows he saw light reflect off something. Gavilan reached out, picking up the shield where it must have been for untold ages. Heavier than any he had used, it looked old and in need of cleaning, yet at the touch he felt an odd tingling nibble at his fingers tips and rush up his arm.

"Is it there?" Laydya's hoarse whisper reached him.

Shaking off the strange sensations caused by touching the shield, Gavilan joined Laydya in front of the creature, the shield on his arm.

"Dust off the front surface, and face it toward this . . . *thing*." Hearing Laydya's instructions, the creature began screeching, folding its clawed hands in front of its face as if trying to protect itself. As soon as Gavilan cleaned a spot off with the tail of his tunic, he faced it toward the creature. Laydya stepped around to look into the shield, and gasp at what she saw.

In front of them was a hideous creature, misshapen by the evil, which possessed it. What she saw looking back from the polished area of the shield was a stunning young girl with red locks down to her waist. Dark eyes mirrored the tormented soul hidden behind this . . . this thing. Both of them watched as the girl smiled, then heard not the singsong of the demon, but the musical voice of youth.

"Thank you for releasing me of my fate. Beware of Kasadim! He can change anything or anyone into whatever he wishes using the evil magic he has perfected. He sucks their soul dry to replenish his powers. Your's . . ." she added, pointing at Laydya from inside the shield, "he wants most of all. Beware! Beware!"

And then, she was gone!

Both the reflection in the shield, and the creature which had just stood before them, disappeared in a wisp of smoke. Suddenly, Laydya and Gavilan found themselves alone in the Cavern of Kings.

Chapter 17

Gavilan sat with his back against a tree, his ripped tunic in one hand and the shield resting in his lap. After their return from the Caverns, Laydya had bathed in the nearby stream, then curled up on the furs next to him in exhaustion. Damen had disappeared into the desolate landscape to hunt, leaving without barely a sound.

As he began polishing the shield Gavilan found several sets of strange etchings cleverly arranged in different patterns over the surface. After removing years of built up grime Gavilan was stunned to find a warrior's shield of dazzling beauty. The etchings ran around the outer edge close to the rim continuing with more unusual ones in the center to form a unique sunburst toward the edge. Each time Gavilan touched it, his flesh throbbed with the oddest sensations.

Magic!

Everywhere he turned there was some sort of magic around him. Gavilan's face contorted into a grimace. If Laydya had chanced to see his face at that moment, it would only confirmed her knowledge of the contempt he held for such things. Yet, he couldn't stop the quiver that coursed up his muscled arms as he continued to methodically polished the shield.   He couldn't read the symbols on the shield. In fact, he knew there were very few people still alive who could read the Ancients' writings. Until now, he had firmly believed only someone considered cursed could be affected by magic, but with each bit of tarnish he removed from the metal, he found himself linked even closer to the now shimmering object. Somewhere from deep in his soul Gavilan finally accepted that all magic might not be bad.

With that thought he felt the tingling increase as his palm caressed the shield. According to Laydya and Eric, the legends declared Ziocon had been the warrior who had commissioned the shield made and blessed. His own hand had put the instilled the spells and incantations into the careful molding of the shield. It was said that only a warrior who was pure heart and mind could pick up this treasure and be allowed to use it. As if the shield itself actually held a living entity within.

Perhaps . . . just as Laydya had tried to tell him, there was a certain amount of magic in all things around them, both good and evil! Gavilan felt a profound, all-consuming acceptance settle over him. A peace of mind he hadn't felt in a long time followed, one like he hadn't experienced since his discovery of *why* his father had turned against him.

Laydya's reluctance in accepting her gifts, her being different from those around her, all of it suddenly became crystal clear. Without those gifts, she probably would have been raised the same way all those simpering, pampered females he had avoided in the past. Instead, she had been forced to learn how to depend on herself, to trust her instincts and talents because she didn't have a choice. Destiny had decided at her birth the journey she would travel.

No, Gavilan finally accepted that fact deep within himself knowing Laydya was anything but evil. Her goodness and integrity was beyond most warriors he had fought with and he would was thankful she stood by his side. It was a hard lesson to accept but a necessary one. Evil walked the land, but Laydya and his brother where the forces to help him stop it once and for all. Magic didn't have to be the vile corruption that had been drilled into so many since birth. Very few people knew Eric possessed such bizarre gifts and Lord Invor even refused to acknowledge it himself. Every hint of that possibility had been carefully explained away so no one could find a reason for disparaging the potential heir to Dragonslair. Despite the consequences that could be brought upon his family, Eric still had felt driven to what he claimed was a calling to the *Learned* circle. Gavilan was the first to admit a true calling must not be ignored!

He looked down at the sleeping woman lying next to him, her dark, honey-gold hair spread in disarray as she slumbered. Now that Laydya had literally dropped into his life, Gavilan was sure she had never had an evil thought in her life. Raw emotions churned his insides at the thought of anything or anyone ever harming a single hair on her head. In that instant, Gavilan faced the truth.

He could never let this woman go!

Laydya had captured his heart and wrapped her magic web around him so thoroughly, he would be only half a person without her! No woman he had ever taken to his bed had responded in such a lusty, uninhibited manner. All others had but one thought, marriage and with it, wealth and social standing. Never had any of them sought to know Gavilan, the man!

Not until Laydya Valeyrian.

Lately, Gavilan had found he couldn't even breathe without first checking to see if she was safe. Had it really only been mere weeks since Dougal had freed him from the slavers?

His thoughts were interrupted as Laydya whimpered in her sleep. Gavilan set down the shield next to him as he slid down to cuddle Laydya's softness next to himself. Gently, he brushed sweet smelling hair from a delicate ear as he wet the end of his finger to tease the soft lobe. Still asleep, Laydya batted at it away thinking it was a pesky insect.

Chuckling softly he decided to explored this lovely woman in his arms. Instead of dressing after her bath, Laydya had wrapped herself in a linen cloth, making it easy to pull it loose. His breath caught at the sight of a rosy tipped breast exposed to the soft light filtering through the branches overhead. God's blood, how could such a wisp of a girl expertly wield a sword and remain such a temptation. He gently stroked a soft shoulder letting his fingers linger over the curve of her collarbone and held his breath as he watched her continue to sleep.

Laydya moaned softly, and he stilled, waiting to see if she would come fully awake. Restlessly, she groaned again, then like a sleek cat instinctively seeking the reassuring touch of its human companion, she snuggled closer to his warmth, thus, setting him on fire. In the process, the cloth fell completely away, giving him easy access to the succulent nipple he had uncovered only moments before.

Like a moth to a flame, Gavilan drew the sensitive tip into his mouth, his tongue experiencing it in slow, sensuous strokes as he watched Laydya's face. As he suckled like a babe, his free hand trailed down her golden skin to the valley nestled between her thighs. Even in sleep, Laydya's body responded with the same passion as before; hot, sweet, and addictive.

Her softness ignited the fragile thread of control Gavilan fought to maintain. His blood raged like hot lava through his body, his throbbing shaft ached with a need so strong, it sucked his breath away. All thoughts of the shield and its ancient pull were temporarily vaporized by the hypnotic pull of Laydya's passion filling the palm of his hand. With a gentleness so unlike his warrior image, Gavilan released her rosy nipple to begin a slow sensuous assault on her neck.

As he continued his foreplay, Laydya's dream began to change from one of creatures chasing her through deep woods and with overcast moon, to become the waterfall where Gavilan had first made love to her. She could taste the scent of him, feel his hard muscled chest rubbing against her swollen breasts. A stroke across one tip of her breast with his hot tongue brought Laydya fully awake, quickly realized it was no dream.

Gavilan was braced on his elbows above her, his green eyes burning with a passion that ignited an answering fire deep within her. Gently, he began to stroke her softness with his teeth, only this time Laydya was fully awake to appreciate it. Relentlessly, he pushed her, making her seek the release only he could give her. He explored every hidden valley, every curve, with a reverence that stroked Laydya's passion drugged senses. Gentleness belied his strength as Gavilan suddenly flipped Laydya on her stomach, pushing aside luscious hair to leisurely sample the bared nape of her neck. His tongue followed his hands as he caressed every inch of her back, sliding down her small waist, going lower to her hips, and to the sensitive spots behind both knees.

She could only grip the furs beneath her and clench her fingers, gasping for breath as every inch of her body was kissed and worshiped, her heightened senses reeling with the flames he ignited. On and on Gavilan plundered her every secret until Laydya was sure he knew every inch of her by memory.

As his hands continued to hold her hips, Gavilan's tongue caressed the valley of her hips, sliding down to tempt the hidden folds quivering for his touch. His calloused hand slid between her thighs to rest palm up between her and the furs, his magic fingers stroking her bud of desire into rivers of flowing warmth. She was sure the madness would never end but she was flying.

Laydya knew she would explode if Gavilan continued! Never had she felt such burning desire! Unable to do anything but experience the fire, Laydya was totally unprepared when Gavilan slipped his fingers deep into her warmth only to quickly withdraw them. Over and over he repeated it until she was convulsing. Slowly Laydya forgot all but the rhythm he was setting in her blood. Then, there was only the feeling of soaring.

A feeling of lightness suddenly consumed her, freeing her of earthly bonds, which sent her reeling toward the heavens. On and on he drove her until she cried out after one, then another crest. Laydya was positive she would die if he didn't join her!

Laydya was sure they were floating.   There was no other way to explain the electrifying sensations that set her on fire. Reaching around her, Gavilan lovingly braced her against him so her firm breasts were in reach his huge hands.   With a quick thrust, Gavilan completed the link, joining them not only in body, but in soul as well.   Together, they rode the wild, turbulent firestorm to its zenith, sure they would come out on the other side scorched.

Torture!

It was the only word Gavilan could bring to mind as her scent drove him almost beyond control. The softness of her derriere nestled against his throat as he kissed the small of her back, the little indentation at the base of her spine, then trailed down the cleft of her buttocks to taste her liquid warmth as it pooled into his hand.

He continued to stoke the fire even higher determined to hear her moans, despite his own physical pain as he gloried in her response and sure no other woman on the face of the earth could respond to him as this woman in his arms could! All thought was centered on fanning their flames until they both thought they would burst. He could feel her need, her cries muffled by the fur as she moved beneath him. Her small bottom pushed up as he continued his sexual assault from behind, relentless in his pursuit for Laydya to experience total fulfillment before he would even allow himself a small release. He wanted to watch her explode in his hands, his fireball!

Just as Gavilan felt her reach the peak of her pleasure for the second time, he lifted her hips and pulled her toward him as he knelt on the furs. Her warm moistness beckoned to him like a star guiding a weary soldier, and Gavilan guided her back, sheathing himself deeper into that beckoning warmth. He felt Laydya's muscles tighten around him, her body begging for release as he fought his fighting for control. When she started moving against him, all thought of control fled.

They shattered at the same time, their senses melding on a level few would understand and one which Gavilan resigned himself to accept at a level of understanding few could accept. This woman had captured his heart and now his soul. The need to claim her on a magical level just seemed normal at this point.

The revelation hit him just as he eased the two of them down into the furs and pulled a cover over them for sleep. There was time ahead to figure everything else out. For now, he just needed to hold his lover.

Chapter 18

It was some time later, after they both had taken a playful bath and eaten a light evening meal before Laydya noticed how Gavilan touched the shield. She refrained from saying anything about it for a long time until Damen returned from hunting just after dark. The ebony feline immediately approached Gavilan and plopped down with a huff at his side placing one large paw on the shield as if daring Gavilan to tell him remove it.

"Go away, you big tomcat! Be more careful where you put those huge feet of yours!" Gavilan growled, moving the shield to the other side right between himself and Laydya.

Damen hissed, then took a swipe at Gavilan's breeches. Thankfully, those claws were sheathed, or else the dark warrior would have been missing some skin.

"So, you want to play, huh?" Before Laydya could warn him, Gavilan grabbed the cat in a headlock and was instantly rolled off their blanket as Damen yanked back.

They tussled back and forth as Laydya watched closely making sure Damen didn't use his claws. Even a small clip from those nettle sharp weapons could lacerate human skin despite the leather breeches he was wearing. Finally, Gavilan pulled away, obviously winded by their play, and miffed because the panther showed no sign of being tired at all.

Her curiosity about the shield was peaked when Gavilan settled back down next to her, his hand instinctively resting on it. Since Laydya had opened her eyes from the nap, he had been rubbing the fingers of his free hand over and over the strange drawings on the shield.

"Why do you keep fondling the shield as if it was a woman?" Laydya curled against Gavilan's length, so she felt the instant his body tensed at her question.

"There is something about it . . . as if it knows me." He looked befuddled as he glanced at her. "Does that sound strange?"

"If you had ask me that before all this started, I would have answered, yes. Now, I don't have a clue. I've seen some strange things, Gavilan. A be spelled shield is just one more thing to add to the list." She continued to watch him, for even as they talked he continued to fondle the shield. "Tell me what you feel when you touch it," she whispered.

"A strange energy pulses through me. It makes me feel strong, invincible. It's as if it *knows* me!" His voice shook, as if by expressing the thought out loud it might in some way make it so. Gavilan snatched his hand away as the full impact of what he had just revealed hit him. He looked down at her, his eyes troubled. He gently rubbed his thumb between her eyes to smooth the frown that seemed to always be there lately.

"Earlier, while you slept, I think I finally understood how isolated you must have felt all those years while trying to accept the ancient Learning you didn't ask for. It was like the shield's powers cleared away generations of doubt to let me feel just a small fraction of what you had been through, trying to accept what fate has handed you."

"Perhaps it recognizes the warrior you are, or responds to your strength," Laydya replied softly, watching his reaction. "Would that be so bad? Or, maybe you feel the power of all the other warriors who used it before you."

"This whole mess surrounding you reeks of magic, spells and curses like the blood stone Lowen gave you, the weird dreams that come true, and the warnings which come on the wind."

Gavilan shrugged away, leaving her feeling cold and alone. She could feel him withdrawing from her, but she couldn't stop it. Laydya knew a time had come for Gavilan to either accept her as she was with all that encompassed, or turn his back on her and their future.

"Will it never cease? What do we have to do to stop all this madness? Why would the powers of Ziocon reach out to me, a man has never believed in magic?" Gavilan stood braced against a tree.

His bronze back rippled with tension, the energy reaching out toward Laydya. She felt his rage, his confusion, but most of all, the struggle within him to try to accept everything that was happening to him!

"We have to do is find Kasadim. So much of what is at work around us is directly tied to him, Gavilan." The determination in her tired reply stunned him, compelling Gavilan to turn and look down where Laydya was still kneeling on their pallet of furs and blankets.

"We have to do it together Gavilan, separately we will fail. I feel it, here!" Laydya slammed her fist into her breast, the sound echoing into the night. She stared at his stormy green gaze, his feeling of revulsion flooding her senses as she tried to cope with it. No, her mind screamed. Please, don't turn away from me now, not when I need you most!

Somehow, Gavilan heard her silent plea. He saw it reflected in her eyes, in the stubborn set of her jaw, but most of all, in the trembling of her lower lip just before she caught it between her small teeth. Not only did her beauty beckon him, but the fierce need to bring back the woman warrior who had challenged him to sword dance struck at his very soul. Their eyes held, the moments dragging until he finally accepted what fate had given him.

"Aye, my golden warrior, together we can conquer the world!" he whispered softly.

Laydya heard the conviction in his words, but still she held his gaze.

"I will do this alone if I must, Gavilan! If we cannot do this together as one, it must not be done at all!" This would be the only admission he would get from her, her need for his strength and his help. Gavilan knew how much it cost her to admit even that out loud.

"You will not have to do this alone, love!" Gavilan groaned as he pulled her back into the safety of his arms, admitting to himself he would die before let anything happen to her.

For the rest of the night, they slept wrapped in each other's arms, but a foreboding prickled Gavilan's senses, even in sleep. As the night's sultry softness turned to a cool mist, the shield took on a spectral glow only Damen witnessed. The respective waves of its soft radiance settled over the sleeping couple like a sheltering cocoon, bathing them in a magical haze having nothing to do with the moon glow slipping beyond the western horizon. Damen's golden eyes burned with an answering gleam full of uncanny intelligence as he watched the luminescent shell settle protectively over his human companions. The huge cat tentatively tested the slight breeze, his delicate nostrils flaring to catch even the slightest hint of danger. Content that all was well, the sleek, black panther rested his elegant head across his paws and closed his eyes with what could only be described as a satisfied smirk on his feline lips.

Chapter 19

Gavilan and Laydya broke camp from beneath the towering cliffs and ancient trees guarding the shadowy entrance of the Cavern of Kings early the next day with Laydya convinced her dark warrior would remain with her until the end, whenever that might be! Their talk late into the night to plan for any possible complication would only go so far to thwart Kasadim.

With Lowen's instructions concerning a perilous but shorter route which could only be found from the canyon, committed to memory, Laydya prayed that whatever lay ahead would soon be over. She was weary of all the turmoil and uncertainty and Valeyrian Keep and its people needed her!

A wave of terror consumed Laydya as she thought of Lowen, enshrouded in a living death cocoon until this battle was finished, one way or another. Laydya refused to herself to even think of what the Druidess' fate would be if she could not defeat Kasadim, no matter the cost!

The trail was steep and dangerous as Gavilan led the way out of the hidden canyon with Damen scouting just ahead. Several times the horses balked at their riders' silent instructions, unable to trust the path under their hooves. At times Gavilan swore, unable to see the trail. Suddenly, the clouds overhead shifted, moving shadows to clear the way for the weary travelers.

Hours passed before they crested an obscure pass, its existence concealed by outcroppings of boulders and brush that had been undisturbed for centuries. Damen disappeared behind what appeared to be a huge boulder then stuck his head around as if wondering why the others didn't hurry.

Gavilan glanced over his shoulder at Laydya assuring himself that she was safe, then dismounted and led his huge horse around the stone entrance. Laydya followed suit, chilly fingers of apprehension pulling at her nerves.

There was barely room for the horses to fit between the rough granite walls reaching toward the sky and Gavilan's first thought was how it would be impossible to defend an attack in such a small area. Damen's calmness assured him if danger were near by the big cat would surely sense it.

As Laydya led her mare into the narrow opening her thoughts were echoing those of Gavilan. Yet, the apprehension she felt wasn't of danger. Instead, it inundated her with a demand to be wary as if something were waiting ahead, just beyond the safety of the stony crags towering on either side of them. It was no wonder few knew of this short cut through the mountains and used it. Nor would it be difficult to get a huge amount of supplies down the cut in the rocks but during the rainy season any kind of deluge would result in the death of anyone or anything caught at the bottom of the path as rushing water came down the towering sides of the rocks.

She and Gavilan drew relieved shaky breaths as they finally exited the ominous stone crevice to find themselves standing on a wide ledge overlooking the lush, fertile green valleys that were a part of the vast Valeyrian lands. Gavilan came to stand next to her, his arm encircling her slender waist as he pulled her protectively into his warmth.

"We are almost there, love. Soon," he added, kissing her hair as she held him close.

Yes, Laydya silently answered. Soon . . . it would be over!

As dawn's rosy fingers threaded golden strands among the shadows of the valley below Laydya quietly sat by a low burning fire listening to nature slowly waking up to another day. Damen's quiet snoring reassured her that no danger lurked in the receding shadows, but the uneasy awareness of something on the invisible strands of the wind had brought her out of a sound sleep hours before. She glanced over to the pallet where Gavilan still slumbered, and smiled.

The memory of how easily the dark warrior's battle scarred hands stroked her body to exquisite passion caused Laydya to flush with pleasure. It was a constant source of amazement each time they made love, for he brought her not only unbelievable joy, but a union of their souls as well! Gavilan's ability to *sense* her pleasure doubled back to escalate it higher and higher. Their loving was a shared experience, each feeling the other's hunger, and with that merging came new heights of understanding of the unique gift that joined the two of them.

Laydya was convinced her dark warrior had no idea of how much Learned ability he also possessed. As she watched him sleep, her only hope was when they came to the end of whatever awaited them they would still have a future together to explore the depths of this rare gift they shared.

The growling of her stomach told Laydya if she didn't eat something soon, the entire surrounding countryside would know where they were. Taking care not to make any noise, she rummaged through their remaining supplies to prepare a merger meal of oatcakes seasoning them with the leftover pheasant Gavilan and Damen had managed to catch the previous day. Hopefully, she would be able to entice her warrior to wake up soon.

Delicious smells of food caught on the light morning breeze, tickling Gavilan's noise and exciting the juices of his stomach, slowly pulling him from the most exotic dream he had ever experienced. He opened his eyes and the sight of Laydya's unbound hair as she pulled it over one shoulder out of her way was a sensuous reminder of the previous night.

The memory of how the gentle sway of the luxurious honey colored tresses felt as the had caressed his thighs and stomach the night before, made those respective areas of Gavilan's body clench with anticipation. As he watched Laydya struggle with the meal, he suppressed a grin. His wanton imp certainly needed lessons on how to prepare food, but he found it only intensified the protective feelings weaving their magic around his heart.

Even though Gavilan hadn't so much as moved a muscle, Laydya sensed his thoughts and flushed crimson as she looked up to meet eyes the deepest green she had ever encountered. His wicked grin only intensified her embarrassment, for she too remembered just how wanton and aggressive she had been the night before.

"Why do you turn the shade of the high sun when I look at you?" Gavilan softly asked, his nude body covered only by a blanket thrown across his lean hips. It wasn't enough to hide the prominent evidence of what his thoughts were about.

"I didn't mean to wake you so early. I thought to prepare us a meal so we could be on our way." Laydya was appalled she couldn't think straight with those startling green eyes staring at her, burning so bright she felt scorched by their heat.

Gavilan threw back his head and laughed.

"Oh, little bird, you amaze me at times. I shall enjoy the next lifetime, exploring all of the hidden facets of you for it is certain I won't discover all of them in this one!" At her outcry of indignant rage, Gavilan's hilarity filled the small glen where they were camped.

She was on top of him in an instant, her strong fists pounding on his massive chest as he tried to wiped the tears of laughter from his cheeks caused by her antics. Laydya was determine to retaliate against him even more when Damen's cough and loud sneeze froze her. She whirled around first looking at the ebony cat, still casually stretched out across from them near the fire, swiping a huge paw across his face, and then to the forgotten meal burning merrily unattended.

"Oh, look what you've done, you beast! I was trying to cook something, and you've ruined it!" she wailed, striking him even harder than before.

"Me?" he returned, a feign look making his thick, black brows rise questioningly.

"Yes, you! If you hadn't . . . Oh!"

Laydya hopped off of him quickly reaching for the source of their argument, but before she touched the hot metal, Gavilan's large hand covered hers.

"Easy, love. A meal is not worth burning your sword hand over." With those words, he quickly used a corner of a nearby blanket to flip the blackened meal several feet from the fire. The flames smoldered for a bit then Gavilan hurried over shoving dirt over it to put out the rest of the flames.

"Now what will we eat? I have used all of the oats and the rest of bird from yesterday!" Tears pooled in her stormy, tawny eyes, pulling at Gavilan's heartstrings.

"It will not be the first time I have gone hungry, and it probably won't be the last." Gavilan spoke as he pulled on his riding leathers and a tunic, automatically strapping his sword around his lean waist. With a silent hand signal, he sent Damen into the forest, then turned to the distraught woman chewing on her bottom lip. He smiled as he gathered her into his arms.

"Hence forth, try not to surprise me with your culinary wit, little warrior. There will be time enough to learn what you need when this is all over." Gavilan stroked her hair, feeling the tension ebb from her as he pulled her closer.

"Why not ready the camp, and I will go see what the forest has to offer a starving man and his maid."

At his last comment, Laydya pushed slightly away from him ready to give him another sound pounding, but the soft smile she encountered brought her up short. Heat rose up from her toes to the top of her head as she recognized the barely leashed, sensual hunger in his emerald gaze.

With a quick hug, Gavilan struck off after her cat, and Laydya had an uncanny feeling that her dark warrior was still chuckling to himself at her expense. She shrugged and eyed the offending meal covered with dirt.

"Well, I certainly hope the forest creatures enjoy it!"

Chapter 20

When Gavilan returned from his foraging, the pair feasted on the fruits of the forest and the cold water from the stream. Once they finished and packed up it was time to begin their journey once more.

They had been traveling for some time without incident until Laydya's hair on the back of her neck prickled. She tried to keep her attention easy but her awareness of being watched sharpened and intensified to the point her skin felt tight and itchy. She didn't detect or sense evil near them, yet she knew they were being followed and watched very closely. Since they had crossed a ridge into Valeyrian lands hours before a sense of being stalked had escalated until it twisted her stomach after the merger meal of berries and roots and it was causing the acid in her stomach to revolt.

There was no scent of danger, just an eerie, symbiotic essence that lingered just beyond the reaches of her abilities, teasing and haunting her at the same time. Laydya located Damen loping just a few lengths to her right. The huge panther paused, as if sensing his mistress' uneasiness, his golden eyes echoing the overwhelming sense of foreboding stalking them. When she mentioned it to Gavilan, he seemed more determined than ever to hurry down the trail.

But to where?

The sun was nearing its midday peak when she felt the first prickling of danger. Damen was staying unusually close, almost under her horse's feet and it was causing the feisty mare to toss her head in agitation at the panther's scent. The cat's satiny ears continued to twitched back and forth, a deep growl rumbled in his chest, stirring the horses into further anxiety beyond what they picked up from their tense riders.

Gavilan was in the lead, and Laydya was determined to stay as close as possible to his mighty black warhorse. The landscape changed from towering trees to sandstone bluffs covered in sparse, stunted brush, and riding down between the tall bluffs was so confining that it made it hard to breath. The tall warrior in front pulled up, looking down at the various paths cutting through the countryside just in front them, trying to decide which would be the safest and fastest.

Laydya was thankful it wasn't the rainy season. High water marks on the rocks just above her shoulders told a story of their own. These dry beds were run offs for the cliffs they had just left behind. Reaching out to touch one of the water lines, she shivered. No living thing could withstand the torrents of water that had made those markers.

"We have to get out of these. It is too good of a place for an ambush." Gavilan's whispered words added to the uneasiness hanging all around them.

Closing her eyes, Laydya reached out on the dimming light filtering into the canyons. Stretching her senses, she felt a stirring off to her left, but recognized it as Damen's strength flowing toward her. Passing it, she directed her silent search down one of the nearby channels, then the other, tasting for any hint of danger.

Nothing but silence met her search. Opening her eyes, she blinked at the glaring light.

"I can't feel anything down either passage. Which direction should we go for the quickest route back to Valeyrian?" she whispered, the sound echoing off the sandstone and doubling back despite the care she had taken to talk softly.

He wasn't looking at her, but Laydya noticed Gavilan had one hand resting on his sword, the other absently stroking the shield as it hung on a strap over his saddle.

When he finally did look at her, Laydya saw something undefinable in his face.

"Stay very close to me. There is something wrong here, but I am not certain what it is!" Gavilan's command shook her.

"I felt something earlier, as if we were being watched, but I can't sense anything now. 'Tis spooky! It feels much like something cloaked or covered, so that my senses can't touch it."

"Do not take any chances," was his terse reply, as he headed his huge black horse into the channel on the left.

It happened so quickly, neither of them had time to even draw their swords. Shadows began to form on both sides of them, changing from mere brush to hulking entities that left Laydya's senses reeling in pain. Without a sound, the shadows transformed into the shapes of men wrapped in ragged cloths from head to foot. She could barely discern where their eyes were, or if there was even a space for them to breathe through. Their hands were wrapped as well, and each one carried either a sword or a strange half-moon shaped weapon. She took all of it in within a space of a few heartbeats, but it was too late.

Just as Gavilan turned to warn her, Laydya screamed.

The horde of shadow men surrounded them, striving to pull them from their mounts. Gavilan began to fight like a man demented as he tried to get to her. She saw several of their attackers throw a net-like contraption over Damen, quickly entangling him as he rolled and fought to free himself.

Now berserk, Gavilan was hacking his sword with a vengeance, his muscled legs the only thing holding him astride his mount. His well-trained warhorse kicked out at an attacker coming up from behind them. The sickening thud of a skull cracking echoed in the small canyon.

It was like a nightmare come true.

But how? she asked herself.

There had been no warning, no taste of these evil creatures on the silver threads of silence when she had scanned the channel. Laydya had no time to dwell on it as her sword slashed out at one of the 'things', the sound of steel kissing steel ringing throughout the dry landscape. The blow caused her arm to sting all the way to her shoulder.

Suddenly, something landed behind her on the mare, and the rotten smell of dead flesh choked her senses. Incredibly strong hands closed around her throat and Laydya slammed an elbow into her attacker's midsection. The grunt of the attacker caused him to bend forward, leaning on her for support and the shocking taste of evil lashed out at her consciousness.

The shadow warrior wrapped a forearm around Laydya's neck, bringing the hilt of his sword down on the side of her head before she could outmaneuver him. Her last conscious thought was a prayer that all of them would survive this, as she watched one of the shadows hit Gavilan from behind as well.

"G A V I L A N !!!!"

Laydya's agonizing scream careened among the canyons, echoing and resounding to the heavens as blackness closed around her, drawing her into its murky depths.

Chapter 21

The war drums beating loudly in his head woke him, causing his stomach to roll and bile to race to the back of his throat. It was worse than any hangover he'd ever had, that's for sure. His head felt as if someone had tried to cave it in and when he felt the swollen goose egg on it, he was pretty sure someone had come close to carrying it off. He tried to open his eyes but for some reason either his eye lids weren't open or he was dreaming. When he finally realized he was awake, darkness surrounded him.   Gavilan could hear screaming, the sound shrill and foreboding, like a small child lost forever in a black hole!

The engulfing black void was stifling, yet a chill hung in the air as if death waited around the corner. With a groan, Gavilan rolled over onto his knees and felt a stabbing pain ricochet through his head again. He stayed hunched over until the bright stars behind his eyes cleared otherwise there was no way the contents of his stomach would stay down. Vowing an oath upon all that was holy, Gavilan swore to kill the man who did this to him when he got the chance!

The scream came again, and Gavilan recognized Damen's agonized cry. Why was Damen making so damn much noise? Then he remembered!

Laydya, oh gods! Where was Laydya?

He tried to stand again and the horrendous pain inside his head threatened to bring the mightiest warrior of the land to his knees in tears. Fighting the ominous void of darkness that waited to claim him and the rolling of his stomach, Gavilan reached out for something to steady himself against and found a cold, wet granite wall less than an arm's length away. He clawed himself up, swaying as he rested his aching head against the coldness.

When he could finally open his eyes Gavilan realized he was in some sort of cell with no windows of any kind. Well, at least he wasn't blind after all!

Gently feeling his way along the cold stones he found no openings or creases suggesting a door or window, nothing, not even a chamber pot. His knuckles finally scraped rough wood on the fourth wall and found what he suspected was a handle. It confirmed his deepest dread, that he was indeed locked deep in bowls of some dungeon in a cell.

"Laydya?" His parched whisper fell hollow on the empty cage.

No sound except the scurrying of small furry inhabitants answered him.

"God Laydya, where are you?" Gavilan lay his aching head against the cold stone, wishing he had just a small fraction of Laydya's gifts. He desperately needed to know she was at least alive. Damen's screams echoed in the dampness, mirroring the torment in Gavilan's soul.

At that same moment Laydya was wishing the same thing except she was in a different sort of cage. She had awakened to bright lights and clanging noises, which had brought her straight up from a soft bed. A girl no older than herself stood next to the draped bed hovering over a tray on a small table nearby. The girl had obviously been uncovering a dish when she had dropped the cover. Now she stood trembling like a rabbit ready to flee from a wolf, her eyes clenched and her whole body shaking. Laydya reached out and touched her, causing the girl to jump as if she had been struck. Her eyes flew open and her mouth opened in a silent scream, but no sound came forth.

Instantly Laydya realized that the girl had no tongue!

"Who did this to you?" she yelled, jumping up and pointing to her own tongue as she spoke. The girl only shook more, flinging her head from side to side in silent denial.

"You must know! How can someone be so cruel?"

"I can!"

Chapter 21

The harsh answer came from Laydya's left, and she swung around ready to behead anyone who would inflict such pain on another human being. Her hand went instinctively to her sword, but it was gone, of course. Nor did she look around for it because her eyes were locked on the man standing in front of her. He was an exact duplicate of her grandfather!

"Who *are* you?" she whispered, incredulous shock turning her deep tan to a ghostly pale color. Laydya was amazed she had a voice at all. In fact, she was having trouble breathing. How could this be happening?

The horrifying reality of seeing Kasadim for the first time quickly dissipated, and Laydya could see a resemblance, but that was all. Thick hair hung just below his shoulders, an ominous white albino shade, instead of salt and pepper color so much like Argon's. Even Kasadim's eyebrows and lashes were bleached, causing his complexion to appear sallow. It was obvious Kasadim was pleased his resemblance to her grandfather had shaken her, but Laydya wouldn't allow the sorcerer's pleasure to continue. This was not her grandfather, no matter how hard the man tried to appear as such. That one thought brought Laydya's center of balance back to normal. It allowed her to finally assess the enemy.

He stood clothed in black robes with red and gold runes etched along the yoke, hem and sleeves, accentuating his pale hair and complexion so that he seemed more sinister. As he began to walk toward her, Kasadim appeared to be floating. Another clever ploy in his attempt to enforce a supernatural fear in his unsuspecting victims. His silent feet barely ruffled the hem of his robe and his hands remained hidden by the long length of the sleeves.

"I am the one you seek, malady. I am Kasadim, Ruler of the Order of Shadows." He bowed as if he were being formally presented to her. This bold attempt at acting congenial made her stomach lurch in contempt. "Aye, I see you finally understand," he said succulently.

With the slightest indication of his head, Kasadim sent the terrified servant girl scurrying from the room. His dark eyes drilled into Laydya as if she were a choice piece of meat ready and willing for his private tasting. The thought almost made her lose the contents of her stomach. An uncontrollable shuddered coursed through her at the coldness Laydya saw reflected in his dark soulless eyes. If the eyes were the mirror to the soul, she was convinced this devil didn't have one.

"Where is Gavilan? What have you done to him?" Laydya boldly stood her ground, but her shaky legs threatened to collapse at any moment. No amount of training from Dougal or Lowen could have prepared her for this meeting.

"Aye yes, your `friend'." Kasadim glided over to the tray and poured two goblets of wine, handing one to her before he continued. She hesitated until he lifted his to take a long drink.

"Your lover is in the dungeon unharmed, for now! And your black devil cat is with him." His slight pause eased her breath a little, until she saw his depraved grin.

Evil lust, strong, black and repulsive, flooded Laydya's mind. It was so strong it forced her to grab the corner bedpost for support. She touched her forehead, fighting with every fiber of her being to block the rush of iniquitous eroticism being forced on her senses in nauseous, undulating waves. Wave upon wave of every vile position and atrocity a human could visit upon another sexually, this monster tried to force images through the barriers Laydya was able to keep at bay. However, many were still able to get through and they were so vile it made her want to scrub her skin until she could peel it away.

"You are truly mad!" she finally screamed, fighting for breath as the amoral visages withdrew back to their vile source. Laydya wanted to fling the goblet of wine back in his face, but one look at those eyes made her remember the girl with no tongue.

"What do you want with us? What do you intend to do?" she hissed through the rivers of pain racking her senses.

"How can you ask such stupid questions? Here you were diligently searching for me, with malicious intent, I might add, and I simply oblige your every wish by bringing you here!" He waved an elegant hand, and Laydya caught a glimpse the claw-like fingernails that tapered to deadly points. She shuddered at the thought of those hands ever touching her.

"Surely you recognize the likeness between Argon and myself! Do you not have any questions as to how that could possibly be the case? I would think it would be difficult for you to murder the likeness of your closest relative!" Kasadim's wicked eyes gleamed as he goaded her. Her legs refused to hold her up any longer. With a cry of despair she slumped onto the edge of the bed.

"So, you do comprehend it! Good, very good! You see my dear, we are related, in but a very small way. Surely you have heard from some of your mother's relatives about this rare trait in your family." He paused dramatically to take a breath, his eyes never leaving her.

"In every other generation, there is born a male that grows into the exact likeness of one of his kinsmen. An uncle, a father, someone will find themselves staring at their exact double." Kasadim waved a robed hand as he motioned to his face. "Of course, there are many generations separating us, but the genetic link is still there. I thought you would be thrilled that you had come to kill the very image of your dear grandfather."

Laydya was stunned beyond words. All she could do was stare at him.

"Now, as for your mission, well . . . we both know that will never succeed, now don't? I have your Gavilan, and his fate is in your small hands. It is as simple as that!" Mad laughter rang throughout the lavishly appointed, high ceiling room. Chilling fingers of fear raced down Laydya's spine, numbing her of any sensation.

His madness was complete, she thought to herself.

"You see, my silly princess . . . I need a queen!" Her eyes grew round as Kasadim came to stand beside her, his hand suddenly snaking out to lift her chin to force her eyes to meet his diabolic and soulless ones.

"What better candidate could I find than one of my own distant kinswoman, several generations removed, of course. One who carries the gifts passed down from her mother's side of the family." His evil snicker squeezed her stomach, causing Laydya to almost lose the fight with her stomach.

"That is sickening. How can you be a kinsman? You died over one hundred years ago." Her contempt was like scalding oil on tender flesh. Kasadim snatched his hand away as if burned.

"Death!?" he screamed. "Do I look dead to you? Do I feel dead?" He made another grab for her chin, missing it when Laydya flung her head to one side. His claw-like fist dug into her right breast, twisting it with a vicious squeeze that almost brought a scream from her.

Almost! Laydya refused to give in to the pain he continued to inflict, even as tears slipped from her clinched lids.

"Now look at me, you spoiled little bitch! You have given freely to that stupid warrior that which was meant to be mine. I can, if I wish, make your life a living hell!" His words spewed out like acid, searing Laydya's heart but not her courage.

Laydya could feel his breath on her neck, but she continued to refuse his command. He tightened his hand, and Laydya was forced to look at him. Kasadim's insane, dark eyes gleamed with an unholy light as he licked his lips.

"I see you understand my meaning." Kasadim's jeering laughter echoed throughout the darkening room. He cruelly pulled her up from her perch on the bed, his clawed fingers settling around her throat with a gentle squeeze.

"You will strip, now!" he ordered succulently, his eyes raking her trembling body with anticipation. His throaty command left her no room to argue. Fear and rage kept Laydya immobile, but the look in his eyes told her she had no choice. Clearly he would rip the cloths from her body if she hesitated one second longer than he wished to wait. He released her throat, stepping back only a few feet.

Angrily, Laydya began unlacing her boots, trying to make the time stretch as long as possible. She hoped Kasadim would be too interested or too angry to notice when she slid her boot dagger out of its' little sheath, but it was grabbed from her hand the instant it cleared the top of her boot.

Keep your thoughts blocked! Lowen's silent voice echoed in her mind, and tears pooled but didn't spill. Laydya refused to give over one more ounce of pleasure to this madman, no matter how much pain he inflicted upon her. One boot quickly followed the other as she stood, taller than most women, in front of her abductor. Kasadim didn't miss the rebellious look on her face, nor the stubborn tilt of her chin.

"Do you honestly think you can take me?" He didn't give her a moment to answer, but seized her neck in the blink of an eye. With her own dagger, he slowly cut each lace and binding from her, prolonging his touch as he peeled away the layers of outer garments, and then her meager under clothes, until she stood naked before him. He didn't release his hold on her neck, but held her firm as his scalding gaze trailed down her body. Laydya felt demoralized as she closed her eyes.

How could she not have sensed the danger sooner? Why?

"Because I can cloak my minions with whatever means I deem necessary and I can read your thoughts like an open book, child. You have lead me a merry chase, my wanton piece of flesh. It never occurred to me that the Druidess would be able to instill the Learned values so quickly into your intelligent mind. I am pleased she succeeded, though. It will make for hours of pleasure after we are joined as we pick apart the Learneds' treasures and hidden secrets, which will be the way I will defeat them, in the end!"

Laydya's eyes widened as she realized what he had just told her. If Kasadim were to succeed, the impact of his actions would be staggering. Subtly fighting for control of her emotions, Laydya managed to block the torrent of feelings rushing through her. The instant she was successful, Laydya saw the sorcerer's eyes flare with anger. She closed her eyes against the deluge of hate that emitted from him.

Her eyes flew back open at the touch of a cold talon finger and thumb on her right nipple, the sharp points gently twisting the sensitive peak to a point of agony. Rage consumed Laydya as she struggled, but Kasadim increased the pressure on her throat just enough to cut off her breathing. Laydya had to stop her struggles, or she would black out completely. She had to know what was coming, and she couldn't do it if she fainted like any common female.

As soon as she stopped struggling, Kasadim relaxed his hold. He didn't seem to want her unconscious, just immobile. Laydya watched in panic as he trailed his free hand down her chest, over her flat stomach, and gently swirled the tawny hair at the apex of her legs. Dread and terror filled her, choking and almost making her gag, it was so strong. All she could do was wait for the rape she was sure would come. Her only thought, was what would Gavilan do if Kasadim raped her? Could he want her?

Laydya's sanity began to slip away as he roughly tugged at the hair under his fingers, bringing the once restrained tears coursing down Laydya's pale cheeks.

"Ah, now the bitch decides to show me her tears." Her captor's strange remark brought Laydya's eyes wide open to find Kasadim's face scant inches from her own.

"You see what I can do now, do you not, Princess? I think you will remember this in the future when I make a demand!" With a disgusted grunt, he flung her down on the bed. Instinct paid off as she rolled across the large expanse to stand out of his reach.

"So, you wish to play games, do you? What of your precious Gavilan's life? You risk so much for modesty."

She wanted to scream that they would all die before submitting to his evil, but Laydya couldn't take a chance. The image of Gavilan and Damen, defenseless and possibly chained sprang to her mind. She cursed the fates for letting it come to this. Kasadim read her thoughts, his insane amusement filling the room as he opened the door to her chambers.

"Yes, I see that you understand now. I will leave you to rest and dress yourself. I have other amusement planned for later I hope you will enjoy!" He glided out of the room as soundlessly as he had appeared.

Chapter 22

Gavilan looked up when his cell door was thrown opened. The outside light was a blinding shard into his eyes as the door swung nosily out to reveal a giant of a man standing just beyond the opening. He was sure he had never seen anyone as tall as this man, or as muscled and this one stood two heads taller than himself. The guard silently motioned him out of the damp cell with the tip of his sword. The cold point touched the base of Gavilan's throat, a clear indication his guard meant business. Just outside the cell Gavilan paused, turning to see a strange cage not twenty feet away, with Damen pacing furiously in it.

Without a word, the giant pushed Gavilan. His eyes were still having trouble adjusting to the light, so he didn't see the metal gate in front of him. The giant gave Gavilan another shove, which sent him slamming into the cold metal.

Not used to being pushed around, much less having someone tower over him, Gavilan turned on his keeper like an animal. He slammed his fist into the giant's midsection, but found it didn't even faze the giant. Instead, a cold grin spread across the giant's ugly features, showing he was missing his tongue and most of his teeth.

The tower hulk picked Gavilan up with one massive fist by the front of his tunic and lifted him off his feet. He hung there for several minutes until the giant slammed him against the wall next to the metal door. The bone-breaking jar didn't help his aching head! Laydya's face flashed before him as blackness took over, sending him back into a painless void without a sound.

When Gavilan again woke up again he was chained, spread eagle to a large, upright, round table. With arms pulled so tight he thought they would come out of their sockets and ankles chained, he was stretched without any possible leverage. His clothes were gone and he was covered by only a loincloth, causing the drafty air of the huge hall to raise the hairs on his skin. His giant guard was nowhere to be seen.

Scanning his surroundings, Gavilan quickly took in the opulent trappings of a very old stone fortification. Tapestries covered the mason stone walls from ceiling to floor, their macabre illustrations depicting dark acts of violence and death. Clean smelling rushes covered the floor, but their odd odor tickled Gavilan's nose relaying strange signals to his foggy brain. He shook his head, instantly regretting the act when it caused nausea from the pounding of his head. He stifled a groan as he tried to touch his head but the manacles bit into his wrists, chaffing them to the point of drawing blood.

When his vision cleared enough to see a little better, Gavilan continued his silent inspection of his surroundings. His search stopped as his eyes settled on a table slightly to the right. Again, he shook his head, sure this vision was just a dream!

Laydya sat there, looking as elegant and as regal as a queen!

She was dressed in a flowing cream gown that barely covered her shoulders, molding to her slim form like a second skin down to her hips. Her posture was so stiff, Gavilan was amazed to see the slightest rise and fall of her breast, reassuring him that she was at least still alive. She sifted positions slightly, slowly raising a silver goblet to her lips. The gown quivered with her movements, pooling in silken splendor around her feet as she sat at the table.

He suddenly realized Laydya was trying desperately not to look at him. In that instant, something just beyond his field of vision moved and he tried to turn his head to search what held Laydya's attention. The metal collar pulled him up short the moment his neck muscles tried to move. He cursed, swearing in every dialect he had ever learned.

With his head restricted, Gavilan resumed trying to inspect the room. A huge stone ceiling towered above them, with dark sinister looking arched ceilings, which was probably why the huge room was so cold and damp. It was apparent that there seemed to be a landing of some kind circling two sides of the room near the ceiling, which indicated other floors rose above. This had to be an old castle of some kind but his memory just couldn't pull up any at the moment.

Torches along the walls threw the corners into deep shadows, but left the center brightly lit. It illuminated the table where Laydya was sitting alone, stiff and unyielding. From what Gavilan could see, there were only two place settings. His curiosity at his surroundings ended when he heard something drop behind him and saw Laydya jump. Gavilan tried to call out to her, but all that came out was a croak. His neck was so constricted by the collar that his throat was too dry to make a sound. His love just sat there, obviously aware that he was only a few feet away from her

Laydya heard his attempt at calling her, but kept her gaze on the man behind Gavilan. Kasadim stood just out of range where Gavilan's chains kept him from moving so that the madman could observe at his pleasure. After Kasadim had left her, Laydya had tried to rally her spirits, drawing on all the training Dougal had drilled into her. Masking her thoughts so Kasadim couldn't know what was going on in her mind, she had put on the clothes he had demanded.

He is a madman! She wanted to scream, letting go of the terror building inside, but that was just what he wanted! Laydya refused to allow Kasadim win. No one would be safe if Kasadim won this bloody crusade he was waging on helpless people.

When Laydya had entered the main hall, the first thing she had seen was Gavilan, chained and unconscious. The second object had been the shield near Kasadim's chair. Lowen's blood red globe was sitting next to Kasadim's goblet, a silent reminder of all that was at stake if Laydya could not find a way to end the madness! The orb had been dull red when she had first entered the dining hall, but now hummed softly to her as if it were reaching out like a living entity.. The moment Laydya sat down at the table, it began to pulsate. The familiar hum of the orb warmed Laydya, but she didn't make a move toward it.

"So . . . we are all here now, and awake at last I see!" Kasadim moved into Gavilan's line of vision, and the dark warrior had to use all of his training not to show one-minute sign of emotion, not even the shock at the resemblance of this madman to Laydya's grandparent.

God's blood, how could this be happening?

"I see that you appreciate beauty as much as I. A pity you took her maidenhead. It was meant for me and I was looking forward to that pleasure myself!" Gavilan knew the man was goading him, but he still couldn't stop himself from straining against the chains. The effort caused his head to pound more than it had before, the pain causing blinding lights to blur his vision.

"Maybe he just wanted a taste of you, Laydya. Do you think he would enjoy watching us making love for the rest of his life? It could be arranged, you know." Kasadim's sadistic grin set Gavilan's nerves on end.

How Gavilan would love to have his sword in hand, then this son of Satan wouldn't be so cocky. He chanced a look at Laydya and saw the slightest shake of her head. What was she trying to tell him?

Laydya mentally concentrated on reaching out to Gavilan, but she had to be very careful. If Kasadim sensed her energy directed at the dark warrior, there was no telling what he would do to Gavilan in a fit of rage. She kept her expressions cool, except when Kasadim mentioned her loss of virginity, but then Laydya forced it from her mind. She had to use all her untried skill to keep the barbs away. As Kasadim long stayed calm, she knew they would remain moderately safe, she hoped!

She knew Gavilan would feel a strange buzz ringing in his ears. Never having tried to force thoughts into another's mind, she found it extremely taxing. He was such a was strong willed man, but she gently pushed until she felt him give in to her mental demands.

"Gavilan, beware! He is mad, and he thinks to make me his wife!" Laydya watched Gavilan as she sent out her thoughts. No sign of emotion crossed his face. She could only hope her stubborn warrior recognized the danger. Projecting her thoughts, carefully weaving them on the threads of golden candlelight concealed in wispy, invisible shards of light, Laydya tried to warn Gavilan of their peril.

"The shield is near his chair and the globe is here on the table. Be ready . . . . stay alert!" Laydya was caught off guard when Kasadim grabbed her chin, forcing her to look away from Gavilan. His touch was like ice! She cringed from him before she could stop herself.

"Good! The sight of him chained like an animal has had the appropriate effect on you. Now you will see what I will do to him if you don't agree to my demands!" He forced her head to look toward the door across the room, directly in front of Gavilan.

Laydya only had a moment to thank the stars above that Kasadim had been unaware of her silent actions. His painful hold on her chin didn't let up even as the door was flung wide open to reveal a hunch-backed figure cloaked in dark clothing.

It moved like a wraith into the quiet room, it's long robes flowing around it in silence. One shoulder was horribly misshapen and thrust upward at an odd angle. As the specter moved into the light, the figure flung back the concealing hood to reveal a disfigured face covered with burns. One eye socket looked to be vacant, its place occupied by a huge blister. Thin, but clean, straggly hair hung matted to the misshaped shoulders. The hands, revealed when it pushed aside the hood, were missing fingers and twisted into claws from the abuse they had suffered.

Laydya's heart ached with the pain she saw mirrored in the one remaining eye. It was difficult to tell what gender the person had once been since there were no indication from the clothing. All she could think of was what kind of madman would do this to any creature, human or otherwise?

"So, do you like my little show and tell, my lady? I have found actions always speak louder than words." He cruelly jerked his hand away from her jaw, causing her head to swing back around to face him. Laydya hoped she showed the proper amount of horror, for all she was feeling was a killing rage to rid the world of this insane demon. "If you do not do as your told, this is what your warrior will look like within the week as one of my minions."

She couldn't stop the horror as it slammed into her, and Laydya gasped as realization that this creature before her had once been a proud warrior so like hers. The thought that it could happen to her lover was unthinkable.

"Good . . . I think you understand now. Let us forget it all for the rest of the evening and enjoy our meal, shall we?" He sounded so casual it made the bile surge to her throat. It took every bit of Dougal's training to school the emotion from her face.

Gavilan had watched the entire scene in silence. He watched as the apparition glowered at Kasadim, but dismissed it as soon as the thing disappeared. He was still stunned by what he thought Laydya had done, or at least what he thought she had tried to do.

She had given him the location of the shield, hadn't she?

His next thought chilled his body, the possibility causing Gavilan to mentally cringe at the thought of Laydya, alone, against such a hideous, demented excuse for a human being.

The madman truly thought himself invincible.

Invincible? Hah, Gavilan scoffed to himself. Here he was chained, with no visible means of getting at his sword or the shield, and he still hoped to kill the bastard? A deep foreboding settled over Gavilan, making the pain in his head start to throb more.

"Gavilan. . .open your eyes!" A strange niggling thought filtered into Gavilan's aching head. He must be truly going mad, because he was sure he had just heard Eric's voice!

"You did hear my voice, you fool, now open your eyes so I can see what goes on with Lady Laydya! I cannot chance reaching for her!" Gavilan shook his head, squeezing his eyes shut to the magic.

"Gavilan . . . I can help her, but I must know the danger! Blast the stars trust me!" Gavilan opened his eyes to mere slits. He heard Eric's gasp in his mind.

"'Tis Kasadim, Eric, and he has both of us." The thought transfer was hard on Gavilan's mind, especially with his pounding headache. His head began to hurt with a renewed vigor as he tried to concentrated.

"Relax brother, all is well." The ancient healing chant echoed in Gavilan's mind, soothing the pain until it vanished. *"Now, where is the globe?"* Gavilan silently told him, feeling his brother's anger mount. *"I must find an answer, Gavilan . . . I will be with you again soon."* And then Eric's presence was gone.

The meal progressed quietly, with Kasadim carrying on a one sided conversation. Laydya continued to avoid looking directly at Gavilan, yet he could <u>feel</u> her terror as if it were his own. When all of the food had been carried away by two cringing women Laydya had never seen before, Kasadim released her to return to her room without so much as a good night. She fled, afraid to stay a minute longer, afraid that the sorcerer would sense her terror, not for herself . . . but for Gavilan!

Laydya tried to put herself in the madman's place, reaching with logic for an answer to what Kasadim might have planned for Gavilan. She couldn't advance past the shadowy wall of horror surrounding her soul. That wall of darkness met her each time Laydya tried to reach past her terror, toward the comforting light that could soothe and heal.

Chapter 23

Several days passed, each the same as the day before with the same ritual. Meals were taken with Kasadim, always accompanied by Gavilan, chained, watching. The wizard's insulting descriptions of what he planned to do once he had made Laydya his wife sent shivers of revulsion through her is she let herself think about it.

Finally, Laydya was at her wits end trying to figure out a means of escape for Gavilan and Damen, especially since she had no idea where they were even being held. One evening she begged the mute maid to draw her a map of where Gavilan and her pet were being held. The girl cringed, refusing with a furious shaking of her head, and answering in the language of the mutes.

Laydya persisted, finally convincing the girl there was no way Kasadim could find out if she just drew a map in the soot from the fireplace. Laydya assured her they would erase it as soon as she had memorized it. The young girl did so, but Laydya would always have nightmares of the consequences of that act.

Kasadim had seemed no different that night at the evening meal, until he brought the girl into the hall. Laydya cringed at what the monster had done to the poor child. Her child-like face was now a bloody pulp, but worst of all she was missing her right hand, the hand which had drawn the soot map for Laydya.

The young maid stood beaten and bleeding, her eyes vacant, her pale skin even more deathly pale from the loss of blood. Her arm lay cradled against her chest even as blood seeped from the unattended wound.

"You see, my dear! Nothing goes on inside my home that I do not take to heart. Each creature, each man, woman and child owe their lives to me. And, make no mistake, I deal harshly with those who misuse it!" Kasadim's soft, eloquent tone belied the evil Laydya witnessed in his eyes.

You cannot involve these innocents, Laydya reprimanded herself, guilt flooding her. She was truly on her own in this dilemma! She would not forget again.

Laydya had just finished getting ready for bed when she heard something moving outside her door. She still cringed at the memory of the poor maid's treatment, which had all but killed her desire for food. Praying it wasn't Kasadim coming to wish her a belated goodnight she quickly looked around for something that could be used as a weapon. Seeing nothing available, Laydya pulled her Learned abilities around her like an invisible cloak, waiting for whatever came in.

The door opened without a sound, a hooded figure softly glided into the room. Laydya couldn't stifle the gasp that escaped her as the wraith-like figure came farther into the room. As it moved toward her, Laydya began to back away until a soft, feminine sigh stopped her.

"Please my lady, do not fear me. I have come to help, if I can!" The soft plea froze Laydya in her tracks. She couldn't believe what she was hearing.

"You're just a child!" Laydya softly moaned, grabbing her throat in horror.

"I was eighteen summers last month, my lady, before the demon master found me. My name is Sarah." Laydya swore she heard a wistful sigh, but the girl continued before she could comment.

"Kasadim took me from my village, and brought me here to serve him in his bed. I was stubborn and willful, crying to go home to my family and the boy I was betrothed to since childhood. He did this to teach me a lesson and to make it so I could never go back." Laydya thought she saw the slightest straightening of the once straight back, a proud tilt to her head.

"Why do you risk coming here? Sarah, what of the young maid, is she alive? Surely you know what he will do if he finds out?"

"Yes my lady, I know what can happen. The girl you ask about died just minutes ago. I, too, would rather die that serve him, this way, or any other." Sarah spread her arms out wide, then reached inside her long robes.

"I have something you will need if you are to free your beloved." The blood red orb glowed with welcoming light in the palm of the young woman's crooked hand. Laydya ran to her, hugging the hunched shoulders as she took the globe.

"Thank you! How will I ever repay you for your help? And how did you know the orb would be the thing to bring? Why not a sword?"

"Because he cannot be killed with steel, my lady. You must fight fire with fire. In this case, magic with magic!" Sarah's childlike whisper renewed Laydya's determination. She clutched the orb to her as she stared into the one remaining eye. A thought struck her suddenly, chilling Laydya's bones until they ached.

"You did not answer me when I asked why? How can I be sure you have not been sent by him just to test me?"

"Because you looked at me with compassion when you first saw me, and I could read your thoughts when you talked to Gavilan!" Sarah's revelation sent Laydya's sense reeling.

"You have the gift?"

"Yes. That is why Kasadim brought me here, to suck the magic from me. But you see my lady, he could not. For some reason, the Master cannot take what is not freely given, or which is protected." Laydya was stunned Kasadim could be thwarted. It was the first real hint that there could be a way to defeat him at his own game.

"What do you mean by `protected'?" she questioned, afraid to believe in the possibility.

"If you can guard your mind against him, he cannot take your gifts. But if Kasadim manages to drug you, or otherwise convince you to relax your hold on your thoughts, he can invade. You must guard well, mistress. He will not stop until he gets what he wants! That is why he did this to me . . . his anger is . . . an abomination." The bundle of rags upon Sarah's body undulated with her loathing, and her fear. Laydya could taste it like bile on her tongue.

"If you are successful, you will free this world of a dark terror from the reaches of the underworld. I also have a selfish reason, for you see before you how his magic can disfigure and maim. Hopefully, if he is vanquished, Kasadim's evil hold will be destroyed, and I will be once more as I was . . . if God's mercy is kind!" she whispered, crossing crooked arms across her chest.

Laydya's heart ached at the pain and hope in that one shinning blue eye. She reached out to touch the girl, but Sarah drew away.

"Beware, do not fail! For if you do, both you and your Gavilan will pay the price no matter what Kasadim has said! I do not wish his anger on anyone, least of all the Chosen!" With that said, Sarah glided from the room, pulling the door soundlessly closed behind her.

Laydya ran to the bed and sat in the middle with her legs crossed under her. Her first thought was to reach out to Eric. He must be told what was happening. As she concentrated, the globe glowed to a rich blood red. The hum in her head increased as Laydya stared at it, willing all else from her thoughts as she reached and stretched for Eric. Just when she thought she would have to stop because of the strain, Laydya felt Eric meet her part way.

"Laydya, where are you? What has happened to you and Gavilan?" Eric's frantic thought waves bombarded her, causing a wave of nausea to heave her stomach. Her eyes

burned, and her legs were beginning to cramp, but still Laydya held to the fragile link that could save all of them.

"Gavilan is in the dungeon, I think. So is Damen. We are being held in Kasadim's mountain hideaway somewhere just inside Valeyrian Lands." Laydya forced her mental thoughts to reach, gliding and weaving on silver threads of moonlight toward the essence of Eric's thoughts.

"I know about Gavilan. I have been in contact with him for the last hour, but I could not find the globe's source, and you were not picking up anything any other way."

"I have been . . . occupied." She felt Eric's questions hurling across the space between them, but she forced them off as she tried to make Eric hear her. *"I need to know what spells will work against him, Eric. Have you interpreted the rest of the scrolls yet?"*

"Yes, and there are several that the old ones used to contain the rogues of the order. They were discovered after Kasadim's incident. Are you ready?" His anxious thoughts were nearly her undoing. Laydya forced her tired body and mind to stay with what she was doing.

It was a good thing Laydya's uncanny ability to remember verbatim anything she saw, read, or heard, or she never would have remembered the spells Eric sent to her. They were complicated and in a language she had never used before. It seem like hours when Eric was finally finished relating the information and released her from the thought transfers.

"Be careful, Laydya. One wrong sentence, or jumbled passage, and you could hurl not only Kasadim, but yourself into eternal doom!" Eric warned before releasing her from his mental hold. After the troubling conversation with Gavilan's brother, Laydya hid the globe under her pillow. She sought out the sliver of moonlight bathing the room with its soft light coming into the tall windows and stared out into the darkness. The

moonlight had always offered her solace in the past until Kasadim brought his evil rampage onto the land. Now, she watched for atrocities and shadows that would manifest into nightmares rivaling any ever thought of in the past. She pulled the moon's energy toward her, allowing frayed nerves to unwind around the tight cord in her chest and relax the tired muscles of her body. Eric was correct and it would take all of them to defeat this monster, but she had to remain centered in order to fight him.

With a tired sigh, Laydya moved to her bed and slipped beneath the soft linen covers. Her last conscious thought was she was so tired of being tired.

Chapter 24

While Laydya slept, Kasadim sat in the tower room staring at the dark heavens long after the moon's decent below the western sky congratulating himself for his supreme intelligence. He now had the object of the prophecy contained in the room below, her obedience guaranteed with her lover held in his dungeon in chains and her unique pet's imminent death promised if she so much as stepped out of line once.

Kasadim was confident his plans would all come to pass. His ego allowed no other outcome and his meticulous planning for so many centuries had ensured it was the only ending possible. There was no one in the world that could stop him now! He had beaten death, for the second time.

The scream of the panther, deep within the bowls of the castle, echoed throughout the quiet stone rooms. The sound set Kasadim's nerve endings on edge but he refused to let the filthy animal's screams get to him for long. He thoughtful stroked his chin, his dark soulless eyes glittering with unholy light as he planned what wonderful sport the black feline would make to celebrate and prove Laydya was truly his!

Gavilan was going crazy as he was forced each day to watch Laydya eat at the large table with their capturer. After each meal, the giant would appear to escort him back down to his cage and would chain him to the wall. Never once did he see an opportunity to overcome his guard. His meals were brought by the same giant and his only time out of the small stone cell was to watch Laydya and Kasadim. Laydya had not tried to contact him again, if what had happened hadn't been a figment of his injured head! He could only hope and pray they could get out of this alive. What in blazes was she waiting for? Surely they weren't meant to end like this.

As Eric's words floated back to him, Gavilan felt his blood run cold.

"She is not able to contact me, probably because of blocking her thoughts from Kasadim. Somehow Gavilan, you must get to the shield. `Tis your only way to protect yourself from him."

"What about Laydya? That monster plans on making her his queen!"

"I know!" came his brother's worried thoughts. The time and space difference didn't block Eric's fear for Laydya.

"Can you not do something to help her? This madman will kill her if she does not agree to his demands. I know her, brother . . . she will not admit defeat unless he means to kill me!"

"Gavilan, she has to contact me . . . I cannot get through . . . She is strong, so be ready!"

"Then how can you get through to me? Why does that devil not pick up on it?"

"I think Damen's close proximity to you has something to do with it, but I am not sure. Evidently Kasadim does not feel you are enough of a threat right now. He seems to be concentrating all his powers on holding Laydya contained. He doesn't realize that you may have the ability for mental thought travel!"

Gavilan rubbed his aching head. It still boggled his mind to be able to *speak* to someone silently. *"I know how you feel about this, Gavilan. but . . ."*

"No, you can't know!" Gavilan silently swore, his savage snarl felt by Eric, and Damen. The cat screamed, his hissing and pacing a constant reminder of where they were. The conversation with Eric had been hours ago, or was it yesterday? He couldn't be certain anymore since all the days, hours, and minutes ran together in this black hell. His only prayer was that Laydya didn't try to take on that devil's spawn alone!

At the same instant, Laydya was inwardly cringing as Kasadim vented his wrath on another new, tongue less girl he had assigned to Laydya. He had discovered the orb was missing!

"You bitch! See what you have done?" The dark haired youngster who couldn't be more than ten summers old, cringed with arms flung over her head for protection as Kasadim railed at her, striking the thin shoulders and back with a riding crop he clenched with talon-like fingers.

"Get out of here. You have ruined the linen by spilling the wine on it. Your mistress could easily have been soiled. Out! OUT!" The small whip struck again, this time cutting a narrow, bloody line across the girl's shoulders. Her mouth opened in silent agony, her movement's jerky as she shuffled from the room.

"I shall find you!" the madman roared up at the ceilings. "The cursed Druids could hide anything, but my power is mightier! You cannot hide from me long!"

Stunned by his ranting, Laydya forced herself to remain absolutely still least he be reminded of her presence. Her mind whirled as she considered his insane ravings, a flicker of hope igniting to smolder in her heart. Kasadim believed the orb held separate power. He *believed* it, beyond everything else!

It didn't matter that the orb responded only to the person who was bonded to it. In the insane sorcerer's mind it held power against him and that power could be turned against him. If so, it could be used to destroy him!

"I will transform them all into creatures! The mindless twits. How could they lose something so important!" He sent a goblet flying across the room, his face a mirror of his satanic soul.

"May I be excused, My Lord? I feel very tired at the moment." She kept her eyes downcast lest he see the deception in them. She was actually terrified of what he might do to one of the maids and she didn't want to be around to see it. The huge rooms became quiet with only the occasional scurrying of feet as servants rushed about unseen, the tension in the air thick enough to cut with a dagger. Laydya shivered, sensing the unleashed evil radiating from Kasadim toward her in waves of revulsion. When he finally turned back toward her direction, his handsome face was calm, almost beautiful in its composure.

All except for those eyes!

Laydya cringed as that satanic gaze focused once more on her.

"You look quite lovely tonight, my dear. `Tis good the moon will be high tonight, for I find myself chaffing at waiting any longer for a taste of you." His pale blue eyes felt like daggers as they raked her from head to toe.

She shivered, revulsion churning what little food she had managed to eat into a torrent of cramps, causing her stomach to heave. Laydya forced all thought from her mind, frantically remembering what Sarah had said.

"Ah, you look so serene, so chaste! But we know better, do we not?" Before Laydya could stop she flinched as he reached out, running a talon finger over a bare shoulder. "Such beauty wasted on a cold innocent. If your lover had been someone with an ounce of mystic ability I would have made his death even slower, more agonizing that even hell could offer. As it is, he is a lucky man. His death will last only as long as he breathes." At her shocked look Kasadim threw back his head, an unholy laughter erupting from the bowls of darkness within his chest to turn Laydya's skin to invisible ice.

"Yes, my lovely Druidess, he will die after I have claimed you, body and soul! It is my ultimate gift to you, to make you watch his torment after I have taken from you what you freely *gave* him!" His hand closed around her aching throat, causing Laydya's breath to come in gasps.

"Now, go to your chambers. There are things I must see to." Kasadim flung her away as if she were an old rag. It took every ounce of Laydya's training to catch herself before hitting the hard dirt floor.   She didn't wait to see what Kasadim's reaction was, as she fled up the stairs as quickly as possible.

Shouts and curses followed her to the second floor as Kasadim issued orders that the orb be found at once upon penalty of death. His superior arrogance refused to even consider that Laydya might try to thwart him.

The moon would be in position tonight! Eric's warnings flowed through her, the prophecy becoming an even heavier burden because too much was at stake. Failure meant death for not just herself but everyone she held dear. Tonight would be the only chance she would have for the incantations Eric had uncovered needed the full force of the moon's light to encapsulate and contain Kasadim's magic!

Tonight, the moon would seem to join with the dark, shadowing part of its glow that normally stuck terror into the hearts of peasant and noble alike. An eclipse that would strike terror into the most sturdy of hearts, no one ventured out into the darkness afraid the souls of the damned reach out to claim living flesh.

Lowen had called it nonsense when last it had occurred, explaining that it was nature's way of setting everything to rights. Evidently the Druidess was correct. Eric had found passages in the old scrolls referring to past occurrences, lending extra power to the art for which the Druids had dedicated their lives.

Laydya again pondered how to lure him into the right spot at the right time. Eric had said Kasadim must be standing in the moonlight, in the same room with her, if the charms were to work to their full strength. She must be holding the globe, her own blood palmed beneath it in plain sight for him to see.

She pulled the globe from its hiding place and placed it on the window seat in the moonlight. Rummaging through the chest at the foot of the bed, Laydya looked through the beautiful clothes that her jailor had deemed appropriate for her to wear, frantically searching for something enticing enough to lure him to her near the window.

Laydya's search ended when she found a diaphanous crimson gown with long sleeves and a very low neckline. The scooped neck of gown revealed a fair amount of cleavage, yet the gossamer transparency beguiled the viewer into false expectations with its lining being the same color as her skin. It hugged her slender frame, allowing the viewer to use his imagination.

Eric had said once she began the chants Kasadim would not be able to move. She only hoped he was right! If not, Laydya was sure she and Gavilan would be dead before this night ended.

Laydya mentally reached out with her thoughts, seeking Sarah. She encountered a radiant softness, and knew instantly that it was the purity of Sarah's soul that she felt. The disfigured girl was close by, and the answering confidence was a balm to Laydya's frayed nerves. She was astonished at the strength with which the girl silently answered.

"Yes my lady, you call?" The childlike thoughts were as soft as her voice had been. Laydya marveled that she could remain untouched after all she had suffered.

"Somehow, you must quickly take the shield to Gavilan. Is there any way you can help him and the panther get free? I need them in my chamber at the height of the moon's journey!"

"What you ask is difficult, but I will find a way. Be careful my lady, for Kasadim will not take kindly to betrayal."

"Have faith, little one! If all goes well, Kasadim will not bother anyone again after this night," Laydya silently promised, praying she was right.

The child's connection suddenly disappeared, leaving an empty void when Laydya tried to locate her. She could only hope that nothing had happened to Sarah because she was Gavilan's only chance! Laydya had to have him there with the shield once Kasadim was immobilized. She silently reached out for Gavilan on the interweaving of moonbeams, searching for his thought patterns.

"Gavilan, help comes. She is called Sarah, trust her," she silently told him, hoping it would be so. She didn't have time to explain more and could only hope that he didn't balk when he saw the disfigured waif. Laydya could hear her jailor cursing as he stomped all the way up the grand staircase.

It was almost time.

Chapter 25

Gavilan felt the soft touch of Laydya's mental caress and finally understood his lover's warning before it suddenly vanished. Who the devil was Sarah?

He didn't have long to wait as the door to his cell slowly began to open. A tortured creature stood at the opening before moving to the wall to unchain him and motion for him to follow it out. He didn't have to be asked twice.

As soon as his eyes adjusted to the light outside his cell, Gavilan was stunned to see the giant slumped against a far wall. Turning to the disfigured waif at his side, he started to ask how, when he saw the shield behind the door.

"The guard will not trouble you any more tonight and with the sunrise he will not remember any of his service to the master." The cloaked figure said, turning to pick up the shield. She held it out to him. "You must hurry, warrior. Kasadim goes now to your Laydya's chambers. She needs you and the shield if she is to destroy him." As she whispered, Sarah moved over to the cage and released Damen. The huge cat moved to slither beneath her hand, rubbing himself against it in what seemed to Gavilan like gratitude.

"But how can she do it alone? I need a sword so I can help her!" He cursed as he took the shield striding over to take the guard's sword from his sleeping hand.

"You fool, do you not understand it yet?" the shrouded figure softly cursed! "He cannot be killed with your damn sword! He can only be defeated with the same magic he wields!" When Gavilan turned back with the sword in one hand and the shield on his other arm, his rescuer was gone!

Laydya trembled as she heard Kasadim approach the door. He had stormed past her door only moments earlier continuing up the stairs to what she presumed was a tower. With a sure quick stroke she sliced her palm with a shard of the earthenware bowl she had broken just moments before, letting the warm blood pool in her hand. Seeing the crimson liquid gently seethe from the wound, Laydya knew there was no turning back.

A shuffling sound from above was followed by footsteps on the stairs, then all was quiet. Laydya sensed him just outside the door and it took absolute concentration not to scream as the latch lifted.

Her nerves were stretched to the point of breaking and her stomach rolled as tension coursed through her. She fought to control it so the only thing Kasadim saw as he entered her chambers was a serene picture without even a hint of her torment.

She would present him the illusion of the loveliest maid he had ever seen she stood near the window in the flowing crimson gown, which she knew hugged her slight curves. Laydya had brushed her long hair until a luxurious shine almost gleamed from the moonlight shining upon her head as it fell almost to her waist. The high moon framed her in the window, it's light flooding into the room spreading like a carpet around her so that she knew what it was Kasadim thought he saw – his queen ready to accept his dictates.

If he had known Laydya better, Kasadim would have seen the determined set of her jaw, the blaze of hate in her glittering eyes. Instead, his madness blinded him to what he believed was a vision of loveliness created just for him, which he had plotted and struggled to attain in his unholy scheme to achieve the power he craved.

With a satanic grin Kasadim moved to the table where the wine waited to be poured. He first filled one goblet, then another. Holding both goblets, he turned to Laydya.

"Come Princess, let us drink to a night of magic and lust."

Laydya stood still. She had to make him come to her.

Her knees felt like water, and Laydya was sure if she moved one-step, she would collapse. She couldn't let him see the orb held behind her back in her left hand, palm up, glowing in a small pool of her own blood. If he saw it or detected it in any way, Laydya knew all was lost. Instead of answering him, she simply held out her right hand for the goblet.

Her silence seemed to intrigue Kasadim, lulling him forward by his all-consuming lust. At the sight of her outstretched hand, he smiled.

"So, you want to enjoy the moonlight first. Such a romantic . . . but soon that will all change, Princess. I promise you that." His insane grin was nearly Laydya's undoing as he began to walk toward her.

I have to wait until he is completely surrounded by the moon's light, I must stay still.

Laydya continued to chant the litany, over and over in her mind, forcing a block from any outside presence so he couldn't sense her intent. As Kasadim drew nearer, the moonlight pooled around him, surrounding him in its silver glow. He placed the wine goblet in her outstretched hand, his cold fingers deliberately caressing hers.

She dared not look at him as she appeared to take a small sip of the wine. Laydya could smell an odd scent rising from the wine, and instantly knew he had planned to drug her. The thought strengthened her anger, and her resolve.

Closing her eyes, Laydya concentrated on the chant Eric had sent to her on silver threads of light, a promise of hope, or death lest she fail. When she opened them again, she gave Kasadim a satisfied smile and began to chant the spell.

Mystics and moonlight, spells and runes,
On this night ye shall meet thy doom.
Evil and Death has been your throne,
Smoke and Hell Fire shall be your tomb.
Never again shall ye roam the earth,
Condemned to eternity for your deeds to man.
Mystics and moonlight, spells and runes,
Vaporize thy spirit upon my command.

As Laydya began the first words of the chant, Kasadim's eyes widened in disbelief. When she held out her other hand with the glowing red orb in her palm of warm blood, he turned deathly pale. Thankfully, Eric predictions had been correct.

The moment she began the chant, Kasadim's voice had been silenced, as he was rendered incapable of moving a single muscle. He was forced to stand there and listen to his doom. Laydya continued to repeat the chant over and over. Eric had warned her, she could not stop until Gavilan brought in the shield, for it was the final key to the eternal destruction and banishment of Kasadim's powers.

She forced her mind to focus on the chant, fearing he might still have enough power to filter into her mind. Not once did she waiver from the ancient, powerful spell. Afraid to move even though her arm was quickly tiring, Laydya continued to stare unwaveringly at this demon from the underworld.

Somewhere not far away Damen screamed an ear-splitting wail as he sensed Laydya's perilous struggle to hold Kasadim immobile. She faltered for an instant, and immediately felt a burning sear of pain in her mind.

In the instant it took to draw a breath, Kasadim sent a force so overpowering it sapped her strength. Laydya saw a sadistic smile creep into the wizard's eyes, and she comprehended his power even while held by the chant, was dangerous.

The pain probably would have killed a less determined person, yet it only fueled Laydya's resolve to send this monster to his death. Her soft chanting tone continued as she drew on every spiritualist and telepathic essence around her, rebuilding her mental strength to fortify her energy.

Lowen had drilled into her that every living, breathing organism in the universe contained its own form of magic. Now she pulled those threads to her, weaving them into an invisible armor of energy that took on an iridescent quality as it surrounded her as she stood on the edge of moonlight.

Her eyes changed colors to that look almost like Damen's and held Kasadim's dark ones, unflinching and full of resolve. Kasadim would find no defect in her shields and she watched as his eyes widen once he realized his mental attack had failed. Laydya saw the instantaneous realization of her growing strength flash across his face and felt his imminent destruction surging through his mind.

Chapter 26

That was how Gavilan found them when he burst into the room. He saw his love bathed in the moonlight, a silver glow of energy surrounding her as she stood in a crimson gown that gleamed like blood against her pale face. Kasadim stood transfixed not three paces from her.

Gavilan could actually feel the orb's hum in the stillness of the room and hear Laydya's soft lilting chants echoing within the vaulted expanse of the chamber. He stood frozen, his rational mind unable to accept what he was seeing. He knew the instant Laydya was aware of his entrance because he felt a soft caress against his senses.

"Gavilan, you must place the shield in front of him, so he has to look at himself." Laydya's silent softness touched his thoughts and eased his fears but did nothing for the rage against this madman who stood before him. Without a second's hesitation, he did as she asked.

Damen appeared from the hallway, snarling at the sorcerer held captive in the moon's light. Gavilan watched as the huge cat circled Laydya's legs, his screams and snarls mixing with the chants she never stopped as the almost invisible, effervescent cloud began to weave around Kasadim. As soon as the cat touched his mistress, her chants became stronger, the invisible cloud more dense.

The instant the panther touched her, Laydya felt a renewed force infuse her, adding to the determination to end this madman's reign of terror. Just as suddenly, two other forces joined her, one consisting of softness and light tainted with pain, the other strong and forceful.

Sarah, and Lowen?

Laydya wasn't allowed the time to contemplate how such a miracle had occurred. All she could do was concentrate on the task at hand and pray she was able to figure it out when and if they all walked out of here alive!

She was aware of cautiously moving around the outskirts of the moonlight to stand reluctantly to one side, sword drawn. Damen continued to slowly circle his mistress, his eyes gleaming as he hissed and screamed at the magic so thick in the room now

Laydya sensed rather than saw the shield in place. Mentally she reached out, pulling the threads of the universe's energy toward her so she could weave the final spell that would destroy Kasadim, forever! She began slowly, enunciating each word and phase with care, refusing to chance even the smallest possibility that Kasadim would escape his fate.

> *Ruler of Shadows hear thy doom,*
> *Released from this earth to enter thy tomb.*
> *The Mirror of Truth has sealed thy fate,*
> *Vapor and Smoke shall be too late.*
> *Mystics and Moonlight shall be thy doom,*
> *On this night ye shall enter the gloom.*
> *For mankind this I demand,*
> *It shall be so, upon my command.*

As the last of the chant settled over the room, the moonlight appeared to turn into a thick mist. It transformed again, collecting, changing until coils of silver energy seethed and furled, taking on a life of its own. Swirling and curling, it wrapped itself around Kasadim. His evil grin was turned to a silent scream as Laydya motioned for Gavilan to raise the Mirror of Truth so there was no chance the monster could miss seeing his image within the polished shield.

Kasadim could not move his head and the instant his eyes locked upon the shield his fate was sealed. As the mist formed a cocoon around him, obscuring him from sight, Gavilan continued to hold the shield.

Laydya repeated the spell over and over again, until not one hair could be seen of the man encased in the living, whirling energy. Kasadim was totally concealed from view in a matter of seconds. She was at first afraid he had slipped away again, until she remembered the last commands that had to be issued.

She stepped out from behind the shield, standing across from Gavilan. With steady hands, Laydya held out the pulsating, blood red orb toward the coiled mass. The mist had formed what could only be described as a thin ice-like web around its victim. She raised the orb high in the air, tilting her palm just slightly so a small amount of her warm blood dripped onto the frozen looking web.

As soon as the blood touched it, the cocoon foamed into some kind of growing thing. Gavilan and Laydya watched as foam encased the evil wizard's web, and Laydya gave the last command.

"Evil be gone from this land, take thy black soul to its judgment." She loudly said it, pointing out the window into the moonlight.

In a flash of blinding light, the encased madman disappeared! Gone, as if never in the room at all!

"You have done well, my daughter!" came a soft whisper on the breeze through the window. Lowen's words were a caress to the tattered remnants of Laydya's control. She cried out, reaching toward the moonlight, needing the reassurance that the Druidess was now free of Kasadim's living tomb. Gavilan's eyes widened, because he had also heard the Druidess.

"Yes, I am free. Dougal is here with me, waiting. We will greet you at Valeyrian, for now is the time to rebuild . . . to begin the future

which will be your legacy for generations to come." The Druidess'
presence disappeared, leaving silence and love in its place.

On the soft sighs of the night, Laydya collapsed into a
crimson heap, great wracking sobs squeezing what little
breath she could draw into her starved lungs. Gavilan
gathered her into his strong arms, pulling her against him as
he braced himself against the window casement. Damen
curled protectively around them both, his golden eyes now
calm, his gleaming teeth forming for what all the world
looked like a satisfied grin. It was a long time before any of
them made a move to leave the chamber.

Chapter 27

Ah, enchanted land . . . thy bounty does rebuild,
  But peace comes at what cost?

The Valeyrian lands were now at peace.

It had taken them a full month to return home after leaving Kasadim's lair. As soon as the sorcerer had evaporated into the night, wonderful transformations had occurred.

Most of the tortured souls that had been held in Kasadim's abusive magical powers had resumed their normal form, some unlucky ones had not. Those who were able, returned to their villages, others simply disappeared into the forest. Sarah was one of the lucky ones, her misshapen form had dissolved when Kasadim's evil died, allowing the soft curves of the girl she had once been to reappear.

With no place to go, Laydya had offered her a home at Valeyrian Keep, and Sarah had graciously accepted. At first, Gavilan had been livid, refusing to even discuss the idea. However, Laydya had been adamant, and when they rode away from the nightmare fortress Sarah was with them.

They found Laydya's home in shambles, the once rich tapestries shredded, the many huts and lodges burned. The few people that had remained were so demoralized, they hadn't believed it could be Laydya until they saw the panther striding by her side. With a roar of recognition, they shouted Lady Laydya Valeyrian's name, a chant to welcome her home.

For a full month after returning, Laydya's nightmares of Kasadim, of demon wolves and shadow warriors haunted her, causing her temper to flare at every turn. She would wake in the night, screaming and clinging to Gavilan, drenched in sweat as she fought the same battles over and over. Gavilan would hold her, soothe her nerves as the demons disappeared, but each time she demanded his lovemaking. It was the stormy passion she used to drive away the horrors of her dreams and then she would fall into an exhausted sleep until dawn. As this cycle continued, Gavilan became withdrawn and preoccupied, snapping at his men they had gathered together on the journey home. The soldiers knew their leader very well, giving him a wide berth when he was in one of his rages. Everyone noticed it, but no one would dare broach the subject.

Dougal had tried once, but only once. Gavilan had flown into a rage and challenged a couple of his men to the training field. It wasn't until he had calmed and realized what he had done that he had stopped and turned, stomping out with the panther at his side. Lowen had been watching from the sidelines and could only shake her head, chuckling to herself with a sad look in her dark blue eyes.

It was Sarah who had finally found him with Damen, Gavilan's mood as black as the cat beside him as he watched the accent of moonrise. The once deformed girl appeared like a lovely ghost from nowhere, standing beside Gavilan without a word, until he was forced to acknowledge her presence. Without knowing the how or why, Gavilan found himself tell her about Laydya's nightmares, and what it was doing to both of them.

"You should have come to me sooner," she admonished him. Sarah took him to her lodge, which Gavilan had ordered built for her near the edge of the forest once they had moved back. It seemed Sarah was much like his lover, needing her peace and quiet most of the time.

"Use this as a lotion, rubbing it into Laydya's skin after her bath. It will naturally calm her, but it will also heal the scars tearing at her soul." Sarah placed the small earthen jar into his battle-scarred hands, taking care not to touch the dark warrior. When he grasped her hand in gratitude, she flinched.

"I apologize, Sarah. Laydya told me how you dislike having anyone touch you. Have you spoken to Lowen about it?" he offered, watching her like Damen did who had followed them to her cabin and now sat comfortably at her feet.

"Yes," Sarah said with a smile that lit her dark brown eyes. "The Druidess has assured me that it will pass. It will just take time."

"If you need anything at all, you have only to ask. You know that, I hope!" he growled, handling the small pot with reverence.

"I know, my friend. Go now, see to Laydya. She has need of you now more than ever. Be gentle with her, for the fears she now fights are ones she is afraid to face in the present rather than those that haunt her from the past." She gently shoved him out the door, and Gavilan was amazed that he even allowed her to do it.

He was amazed at how well the balm worked and Gavilan was so thankful, he gave Sarah a fine horse and cart. She used it to check on the villagers, using her healing knowledge to win them over one at a time. Damen had taken to staying close to the newcomer whenever she went out of the keep, yet he always returned to his mistress. Laydya found it charming and satisfying to know Sarah now had a home and the protection of a family.

With the turning of the season, finally, Gavilan and Laydya found peace. Their passion for each other grew, but without the nightmares to mar it. Laydya began to heal, her body regaining its glow and her mind getting the rest she so desperately craved.

Gavilan was continually amazed at his little warrior's determination to learn about everything she could. He never knew what to expect next. One minute she could be found cleaning a tapestry and the next, polishing her sword, whichever suited her mood. Sarah taught her how to use herbs to ease the pain of the sick and how to sew, and Laydya had finally found a friend her own age she could confide in.

Chapter 27

The spring after the return to Valeyrian, a wedding feast took place. Everyone took part as Dougal and Lowen repeated the sacred vows that would bind them together for this lifetime and the next. The feasting lasted for two days, as was the Druid custom, and Laydya watched the couple with a mixture of sadness and love as they graciously accepted small gifts from well-wishers.

"Why the long face? Are you not happy for them?" Gavilan teased, coming up behind Laydya to pull her close.

"Of course I am happy for them! What a terrible thing for you to say!" she whispered, reaching down to gently pinch his arm. "'Tis just so . . . " Laydya stopped, unable to put her sorrow into words.

"What, my lovely warrior?" Gavilan turned her toward him, amazed to see tears streaming down Laydya's pale face. "Are you having dreams again, Laydya? Is that the cause of your sadness? You are either laughing and bounding around the Keep like a girl without a care in the world, or sad as a sparrow who has lost her brood. What in the name of all that is holy is going on?" He gently shook her, expecting an answer.

Laydya looked up at him, unable to voice the fear that had been growing inside of her for weeks now. When would he become bored and leave? When would Invor summon his son back to Dragonslair, demanding that Gavilan take up his responsibilities?

Each night he came to Laydya's bed, giving and receiving the love meant only for him. And each day, Laydya felt the icy threads of dread thicken around her heart for the day when she would have to watch him ride away from her, forever.

"'Tis not nightmares that haunt me, love. Just a touch of something that sours my stomach now and then, causing my emotions to run rampant. Fear not, all is well." Laydya pulled her Learning about her like a veil, willing Gavilan to see what he wanted to see . . .a content leman willing to serve her man whenever she was needed. It mattered not that she was heiress to a great estate, or that he was heir to an even greater one far from Valeyrian Keep. For as long as he stayed, Laydya clung to the memories they made each night and day, storing them away against the time when those memories would be all she had left of her dark warrior.

There was no way she could explain the dreams of the babe she might carry or the future that she saw just out of her grasp. If he was the heir of Dragonslair then those dreams would remain with her and the babe would be raised at Valeyrian Keep. There was no other option and Laydya refused to force Gavilan to accept any other. He had lost too many years with his father as it way. He deserved to have his family, no matter the costs.

The feasting had only ended the day before when a messenger arrived, bearing no coat of arms and announcing an unexpected guest was on his way to Valeyrian, requesting a place to rest. Laydya noticed a strange exchange between Dougal and Gavilan, but neither man would explain. She tried to question Lowen about it, but the Druidess only smiled, patting Laydya's hand.

"You will see, my child, trust the fates. You seem to have forgotten that there are many things that are out of our hands." With that sage advice and a suspicious chuckle, the Druidess left the Keep for the lodge Dougal and Gavilan had finished just before the wedding and she hadn't returned. Their visitor was supposed to arrive in two days' time, whether she wanted him to or not. Laydya wasn't sure she was ready for this, but both men had told her she had no choice.

While everyone prepared for the visitors to arrive, Laydya contemplated what Lowen had said. Fate, yes, it had decreed many things.

She looked up at the man she loved more than life itself, and marveled that he did, indeed love her. The only thing marring her complete happiness was their future. She knew Gavilan loved her, the passion and fire they shared was beyond anything either of them had ever felt before. He hadn't said the words, but Laydya felt it, that place deep within him no other woman had ever entered, his heart of hearts. She sighed, wishing the visitors would go away so the short time they had together would remained unscathed.

It was early the next day, when Laydya's world began to come apart at the seams. She had planned a picnic for just the two of them, when Dougal interrupted it as soon as the approaching assemblage was sighted.

"Are you going to tell me who our guests are?" Laydya softly questioned. She gently took a very masculine nipple between her teeth, holding it hostage as she stared into his emerald eyes.

Gavilan's breath caught at her hot look, but he still shook his head even as she gently bit down. His growl was her only warning as Gavilan lifted her off of him.

"Why the mystery!" she yelled, hitting him hard against his chest with her fist.

"It is a surprise . . . not a mystery." Gavilan rose quickly, throwing her clothes at her head. "Get dressed, or do you intend to make your first official appearance as hostess dressed as you are?" His only answer was a boot hitting him in the backside.

Laydya fumed, vowing she would get to the bottom of this secret. Everyone knew how much she hated secrets and especially something as important as guests arriving. She was getting damn tired of Gavilan's stubbornness about their future, too. She gently touched her stomach, remembering the dream from several nights before.

Gavilan's babe . . . dark haired and green eyed, lying in her arms, suckling at her breast. Laydya's nipples tingled at the thought, but she pushed it away. Yes, her stubborn warrior had better come around soon! She wanted that babe from her dream.

Gavilan looked very respectable in his fawn colored tight breeches and rust hued tunic as he stood in the huge hall before the hearth. He had insisted Laydya wear one of her new gowns and by the dagger throwing looks she was slicing him with, Gavilan knew there would be fireworks later. Especially after Laydya found out who their guest was!

He knew she had been consumed with the huge task of returning Valeyrian lands back into a semblance of normality. Laydya had raved that gowns just got in the way, and Gavilan had relented. How was one supposed to scrub soot from a wall in one of those dainty things she had raged? But enough was enough, as far as he was concerned.

Laydya was thinking much the same thing as she looked down at the wonderful gown. She had only worn them in their room, finding they enticed Gavilan as nothing else could other than bare skin.

No, she corrected herself . . . her room!

Gavilan still had refused to sleep all night in her room, insisting he return to his own before dawn. They had argued countless times over the point. It didn't make any sense, she had told him! Everyone in the castle knew they slept together at night, so why he demanded to have it his way was beyond her comprehension. As she looked up at him, Laydya was reminded of just how stubborn this man of hers could be!

An enormous commotion outside the large double doors drew Laydya's thoughts back to her unwelcome guests. She wasn't ready to take on the responsibility of hostess, but since there seemed to be no way to avoid it, she started toward the doors.

"Laydya, come here." Gavilan's soft command caught her off guard. She turned a questioning glance at him, but he just crooked a finger at her to come to him.

"Gavilan, not now!" she whispered loudly. "Can you not see I have to meet our guests!" He just motioned for her to come to him. Stomping over to him with hands on hips, Laydya's tawny-gold eyes shot hot daggers up at him. Before she could say a word, Gavilan grabbed her around the waist and pulled her into his massive arms.

Laydya beat against his chest, but it was like hitting a stone wall. When his lips captured hers in a searing kiss she stopped her struggles. Gavilan lifted his head to look at her face, her eyes reflecting the earthy shades of gold and bronze he loved so much.

"I love you, princess. I hope you remember it later," he whispered as he kissed the bridge of her nose.

"Gavilan, you have the oddest look . . .," she chided, but the look in his eyes stole her breath. "Oh Gavilan, why now?" Laydya groaned. Her eyes told him she only wanted to escape to her room to continue their interrupted lunch activities. "I think I will have Dougal beheaded for this!"

"If I'm lucky, he's the only one who will be missing his head by the end of the day, woman!"

Gavilan only chuckled at her oath as he set her back on her feet. Tightly clasping Laydya's hand, he led her to the doors. Just as Gavilan grabbed the massive portal to open it there was a loud oath and a thud against the door. It swung open with a resounding smack, striking the wall behind it as

Dougal came sailing into the hall and landed on the hard stone floor.

"That is for letting her go off in the first place!" boomed a man's voice from just outside the open doorway, and Laydya turned deathly pale.

"Grandfather?" she murmured.

"Aye . . ." came Dougal's painful answer. He was sitting on the floor, rubbing his jaw and grinning like a fool.

"Oh no, what next?" she cried.

"And you missy! Who is this swine who thinks he can sleep with my granddaughter without marrying her first? I told you about these fortune hunters, did I not?"

Chapter 28

The owner of the booming voice moved to stand in the entrance, leaning against the massive doorway. Argon of Falconwood stood as tall as her Gavilan and at the moment, appeared to be in a fine rage. His steely blue eyes drilled into the couple as he crossed his thick, solid arms across his wide chest. Dressed in long woolen tight breeches and fur boots ending at his knees, Argon's shoulders looked wider than usual with his scarlet fur lined hood folded back from his thick neck. Gray hair brushed his collar, and his neat beard accentuated a very stubborn chin.

Laydya corrected her earlier thought. He wasn't in a rage . . . he was livid!

She turned horrified eyes toward her grandfather, as his words sank into her stunned brain. Humiliated to the depths of her soul, a feral scream like one from Damen filled the hall.

"Why do you not just scream it to the rest of the world?" Laydya picked up the hem of her gown and ran toward the stairs. Turning back to where the three men stared at her, she yelled, "If the three of you value your lives, you will not speak to me again in this lifetime . . . ever!"

Laydya ran the rest of the way to her room, sobs trailing behind her as she slammed her bedroom door. The resounding boom could be heard all the way in the great hall. Gavilan flinched at the sound. Rounding on the older man that had just arrived, his angry eyes took on a dangerous light.

"Could you not have been a little more gentle with her, Argon? 'Tis not her fault we haven't stood before the priest yet, it is mine. I wanted your blessing before proceeding."

"Ah whelp, you haven't changed a bit, have you? Not since you first came to Falconwood to foster with me."

Argon slapped Gavilan on the back, then wrapped him in a massive bear hug. "I have missed you son, more than you could ever know."

That admission wasn't lost on Gavilan. Argon had always shown his love without restraint to his foster sons. Gavilan looked into crystalline blue eyes, seeing the slight moisture in their depths.

"I knew you would want to be here, Sire. I haven't mentioned to Laydya about knowing you." Gavilan whispered.

Argon saw the mixed emotions in the younger man's face. He knew well enough how fast Laydya could turn her fiery temper onto whomever she felt had wronged her. He was in a quandary how to solve this problem without doing more damage to her pride, which could be formidable. A woman's hurt pride made a damn bad start for a marriage.

And it was a marriage he had come for!

"Come, fill me in on what has transpired since last I saw you, and explain this foolishness I hear about the mad wizard!" The two men ignored the grinning Dougal, who motioned for the servants to prepare a snack. It looked like it would be a while before anything more was done about the situation.

"Laydya . . . open this door, now!" Argon stood outside Laydya's locked bedroom, screaming for the third time at his enraged granddaughter. She had refused to talk to Gavilan, declined to take the evening meal with her guests, and continued to sulk like a spoiled child in her room. He was tired of it.

When she still didn't answer, Argon decided to take matters into his own hands. Two of his retainers stood nearby, and he motioned for them to break down the door. Laydya couldn't believe her eyes as her grandfather's men put their two mighty shoulders slamming against it, making short work of the thick door and the sturdy lock bolting it shut. She stood dressed in crimson tunic and dark brown breeches as he stepped over the shattered remnants of her door. Argon thought she looked magnificent.

"So, have you come to yell at me some more, or to tell me you are finally leaving?" Laydya defiantly stood her ground, refusing to show the hurt and betrayal she felt. If she were a man, Argon knew she would have called him out onto the field of honor.

"Neither, I am afraid." He sighed, a long tiresome sound to Laydya's ears, and her resolve slipped . . . just a little. "I have come to talk to you, girl. We used to be able to do that, you know. Don't you think it is time you explained yourself?"

Argon moved over to the fireplace where two high backed chairs were placed side by side. She and Gavilan had often sat in those chairs, talking over the day's events before going to bed, and her eyes grew bright with unshed tears. Her grandfather was settled back comfortably with his eyes closed before Laydya realized just how foolishly she wished she could curl into his lap like she had so many times when a little girl and just cry.

"Why are you here, grandfather?" Her whispered question sounded strained to her own ears, but she hoped he didn't notice.

Then, Laydya's grandfather looked at her. The same beloved eyes she had seen filled with pride over some antic or another she had pulled off when she was small, or with compassion when she felt lost and couldn't stop the tears from falling. With a painful cry Laydya flung herself into his arms, sobbing her loneliness and hurt out into his soft shirt.

Argon let her cry, allowing her vent all the anger and pain she had contained for so long before trying to talk to her. He knew this child of his heart so well, it would be a good match, she and Gavilan. They would temper each other and make each other strong.

Laydya finally dried her tears as she curled on the floor at Argon's feet. When she looked up, she saw his smile and blushed.

"You know, you should be more angry that Gavilan wanted to wait to wed you than at me for storming in here. You should know me well enough by now to know you are the light of my heart." He caressed her head as he spoke, his gentle touch reminding Laydya of her father.

"Aye, but you humiliated me in front of all those people!" she cried softly, new tears forming in her blue eyes.

"And when has that stopped you, girl? For weeks, all of the kingdoms have known where you two sleep. Why keep it a secret?" He watched her closely knowing Laydya would never lie to him. He wanted to be sure this was the right thing for his only granddaughter, even if it was Gavilan who wanted to wed her.

"I love him, Sire. More than life itself!" Laydya's adamant reply was all he needed to hear.

"That is a relief, because tomorrow the priest will be here and a huge wedding feast is already being prepared." At her surprised gasp he chuckled, "It is not my fault you have locked yourself in this room since yesterday. Which one of those pretty gowns will be your wedding gown?" Her squeal of delight was all the answer he needed.

"Now, is there anything you should tell me before this blessed event gets underway?" Argon's blue eyes twinkled, full of mischief, which belied his age.

Laydya frowned, wondering what he was talking about. Argon could see she hadn't the foggiest idea of what he spoke of. Was she so naive as not to recognize the signs, or could Gavilan be wrong?

"Sire, you are going to have to be more specific, I think." Laydya's mind whirled, trying to think if there had been something Gavilan might have left out, which her grandfather wanted clarified. Argon watched each emotion spin across her unguarded face.

"Laydya, are you with child?" he asked softly. Laydya's stunned expression was worth a thousand words. First, Argon saw rage; then came doubt, and finally, Laydya looked at him with wonder in those sparkling depths.

"How could you know, when I just realized it myself?"

"Your future husband is not stupid, child. He told me he was taking no chances. He wanted to make sure I would agree, as if the whelp had to worry about that score. That is why he waited to call me here." Argon chuckled as Laydya jumped to her feet.

"Why that . . . !" Laydya swore as she rose to pace in front of the fireplace. "Why could he not just ask? I thought Gavilan hesitated because he was unsure of his future. He is the heir to Dragonslair now. His father will want him there." Tears pooled in her eyes, her hurt echoing in a trembling whisper as she tried to understand it all.

"I could not bear to leave Valeyrian again, Sire. And I cannot have Gavilan if he must relinquish Dragonslair. It would not be fair to him!"

"Child, the man loves you. Do you think he would just walk away?" The truth hit her then, Argon could see it in her eyes.

"Gavilan wanted to make sure you would agree? He was not leaving anything to fate, so he thought to get me with child so you would have to agree?" His grey head slowly nodded, and Argon saw the fury erupt in her gaze.

"I will kill the man!" she screamed. "How dare he presume such a thing, when I was the one who wanted to get this deed done."

"Do not punish him too much, Laydya. Gavilan simply wanted to insure my acceptance of his plans." Argon couldn't hold back the booming laughter any longer. He wondered what she would do to make Gavilan pay for this, for he had no doubt in his mind that she would extract her revenge.

Chapter 29

Laydya glowed in the warm aftermath of the long day's events. The wedding had been everything she had ever dreamed it would be, Lowen and Sarah had stood by her side, with Dougal standing by Gavilan's. Her grandfather had given her away, completing the circle of loved ones around her. Gavilan's arms held her tight against his solid warmth, a reminder of his pledge to her earlier in the day.

As he pulled her securely against him, Laydya's bottom fit perfectly next to his hardness. His warm breath tease her neck.

"Are you asleep, Wife?" She wiggled her rear end against him and he chuckled. "No, I guess you're not." With that he flipped her around to lay on top of him. "So, was this day to your liking, my love?"

Gavilan had seen her sad expression at the beginning of the ceremony and he hoped she hadn't regretted it. He just needed to hear her say she forgave him for his deception.

"You mean am I over my shock of finding out you fostered with my grandfather? That he was the man you had been talking about when you told me of your foster years with another family?" He could tell she was teasing but still he persisted.

"Aye, that . . . and surprising you with your grandfather's grandstand entrance. I honestly didn't think Argon would do something like that, love. If I had, I would have warned you of his coming. Dougal felt it would be easier if we waited until he got here, but I am not so sure that was wise now."

"You could have told me instead of letting me make a fool of myself," she grumbled as she shoved an elbow into his ribs.

"But, do you forgive me, love?"

"I haven't decided just yet," Laydya purred with a wicked gleam in her eyes. "I'm still not sure if all of this is worth it." Laydya let out what she hoped was a bored sigh. "I need to go and confer with Sarah and Lowen on the morrow, Gavilan. I have need of a potion for dealing with you in the years to come, as well as an aliment I have."

Laydya kept her face void of her thoughts, least Gavilan read the teasing there. Gavilan took her bait so easily. She had only one breath to congratulate herself before she found herself pinned to the bed, Gavilan's face hard and frowning down at her.

"What ails you, wife?" he growled. Laydya struggled for air, as Gavilan seemed to be trying to break her ribs. "Tell me!" he yelled into her face. Laydya's smile broke through, startling Gavilan into silence.

"You're so easy to tease, husband! I hope you learn to guard your temper by the time your son is born. I fear you may age quickly if he is anything like me!"

Gavilan could only stare at her. She was goading him again! His anger fled as he comprehended her words, saw her radiance as she caressed his cheek.

"You are not angry about it?" he croaked.

"Angry with you for trying to make me breed so grandfather would agree to this match no matter what? Or angry because you felt you might have to force the issue?"

"Both I guess?" he sighed. "Laydya . . ."

"You should have told me, Gavilan. It would have made things so much easier," she whispered. Gavilan again felt the weight of his decision, his brow knitting together in a dark frown as he reasoned with himself once again. He found himself doing that a lot with his wife around.

"Hush love," Laydya whispered as she ran her fingertips across his brow. "I will forgive you all, if you make love to me like you just did for the rest of my life." She sealed her vow with a sultry kiss that sucked the breath from his body, silently reminding him of her unfailing trust and love.

Moonlight flooded their chamber as Gavilan guided his new wife once more toward ecstasy's release. Laydya trembled as waves of warm, voluptuous heat washed over her, carrying her closer to what he promised. The moon's journey across the long night was unfailing as moonbeams trailed an invisible path for the lovers' passionate voyage.

EPILOGUE

Five years later

Eric and Laydya sat on a blanket under a huge, knotty shade tree, watching two figures down by the stream. A gentle smile burst into a loud chuckle as Laydya watched Gavilan and Mykal trying to spear fish in the shallows. Her noise woke the sleeping little girl curled in Eric's lap, and the child's bright green eyes sleepily studied her mother.

Sensing that her daughter was awake, Laydya pulled her loving gaze from her husband and son to Myra. As always, she marveled that the twins looked so much like Gavilan, and it filled her with a sweet joy.

"Why do you look so funny, mama? Are you angry with papa again for not letting you fish with them?" Myra's singsong voice broke Laydya's daydreams, and Eric turned to see her tickling his stunning little niece.

"Your mama knows she cannot fish with them right now, Myra. She might fall and hurt herself." A wicked gleam twinkled in the clear eyes of Laydya's brother-in-law, and she knew what was coming before he even said it.

"As fat as your mama is right now, do you think she could pull the fish in?"

Myra took exception to her uncle's teasing, springing up on short, four year old legs to fling herself at Eric's chest.

"My mama is not fat. She is only sassy," she stumbled over the words as tiny fists flailed out in quick secession.

"Whoa love, why do you attack your uncle?" The three hadn't heard Gavilan and Mykal approach. Gavilan grabbed his little, raven-haired tyrant, tossing her above his head in order to save his brother. Eric was laughing so hard he was rolling on the blanket.

Myra wrapped chubby arms around her father's neck as she clung to him, her face a picture of indignation as Eric fought to contain his merriment. Mykal chuckled, watching his mother and uncle, but Gavilan's eyes were watching his wife. She sat so prim and proper, a day gown covering her extended belly where their babe lay safely nestled. Gavilan marveled that she looked lovelier than ever.

In the last five years, Gavilan had watched her bloom into the woman she was now. The past was behind them, their demons gone and their loves very full. His daughter squirmed, pulling Gavilan's thoughts back to her.

"So midget, what made you attack your uncle like that?" His sternness was tempered by the bemused twinkle in his eyes, but Myra wasn't intimidated in the least by her father. She had him right where she wanted him all the time. Wrapped around her chubby little fingers.

Pointing her small finger at Eric, she wailed, "He called mama fat. She is not fat! She's sassy!" she yelled down at Eric, which sent him into fits of laughter again.

Gavilan fought his own mirth, keeping a firm hold on the wiggling little girl. At four years old, Gavilan was continually startled at Myra's temper, so like the quick flash of her mother's. It reminded him of Dougal's descriptions of Laydya at that age, and he wondered just what kind of terror this ragamuffin would become in the years to come.

Her twin brother was just the opposite of his sister. Mykal tried diplomacy first, then he would resort to whatever measures were needed. Both children were the spitting image of Gavilan, and both possessed such a keen intellect, their parents were hard pressed to keep them out of mischief. It didn't help that his brother egged them on all of the time.

"Eric, why do you tease her so much? You know she will fly into a rage each time you do it!" Laydya had finally regained her breath, but couldn't find it in her heart to scold him anymore.

"I know, but she is so much like you, 'tis hard not to." Eric wiped his eyes as he watched his brother and niece. Mykal stood beside them both, and Eric was reminded again of the peace his brother had finally found. The three of them looked so much alike, Eric found himself grinning from ear to ear.

"Help me up Eric, 'tis time for the children to rest, and I feel a need for a nap myself." Her tired request instantly warned Gavilan something was amiss. Searching her face, he saw her wince as Eric levered her up, so Gavilan placed Myra on the ground next to her brother.

"Mykal, take Myra to the nursery and I will see that your mama finds her own bed." Gavilan tried to sound bored, but Laydya took one look at his eyes and knew he had guessed her secret.

Gavilan easily lifted his wife into his arms as Eric led the children toward Keep, their excited chatter fading away as Laydya tried to reassure her husband. Silently, she reached out to touch his thoughts, feeling him open up to her as he claimed her arm.

"Please don't alarm the children, husband. I don't want them frightened. It will be a while yet before your son gets here." She smiled at his surprise, concern tightening his features into a grimace.

"Send Eric for Sarah, she will deliver our son this time, instead of you!" Laydya's laughter stopped the two galloping children ahead of them, both turning in unison to see their parents' heads close together.

"She is talking to him in her special way, Myra. See how he frowns when she does it." Mykal glanced at his twin, seeing her puzzled look.

"What special way is that, Mykal? She talks to him the way we usually talk to her!" The indignant little girl's reprimand brought a knowing smile to her brother's solemn face.

"Sometimes. But most of the time papa doesn't talk that way, he likes to hear the words with his ears, not his mind."

"Oh, well . . . when I grow up, my husband had better like it!" Myra huffed in a grown up way. "Otherwise, he won't be talking to me at all."

Mykal only shook his dark head at his sister's dumb remark. He was positive no one would ever want her since she was too much trouble.   Even his papa said so, and his papa was never wrong. Myra ran ahead, leaving him to look back at his parents again.

He hurried to catch up with Myra and Eric, grabbing his sister's hand and then pulling their wizard uncle faster along toward the Keep. Eric's wizard robes flapped as loud as their laughter, and it filtered back to Gavilan and Laydya.

"You are sure it will be easier? I don't think I could bear it if it went like the birth of the twins." Gavilan's concern made Laydya snuggled into the circle of his arm, searching for some way to reassure him. She understood his worry all too well.

When the twins were born they were early with only Gavilan nearby to help her. With the hard labor, Laydya had panicked, screaming at him that it was all his fault. He was just lucky she didn't know how to rain curses down on his head because Gavilan might have been turned into anything . . . even a toad! Afterwards she had blushed at just how vocal she had been.

Turning in his strong arms, she could smell his clean scent and the uniqueness that was Gavilan   With her palms on both sides of his face, Laydya forced him to look at her. She saw the remembered pain he had witnessed with the birth of the twins, the fear that he wouldn't know what to do.

"All is well, love. We are at home instead of a hunting lodge, with Sarah and Lowen nearby to help me this time. The twins came early and neither of us expected it. All will go fine, trust me." Laydya drew his face down to her, her eyes drawing him into the chasm of their passion.

When they both could breathe again, Gavilan held her close and started toward their home.   They were almost to the house when he heard her chuckle.

"I promise I will try not to scream as much, or curse you as loud as I did before."

Hours later, a haggard and pale Gavilan stood holding his new son, while his wife lay sleeping. Sarah and Lowen had already left, and his ears still rang with Laydya's curses and screams, but the small bundle in his arms had been worth it.

Gavilan moved over to the large windows, and stood the moonlight. He looked up into the heavens where the moon crested the towering mountains, and watched a huge falling star streak toward the horizon. Somewhere nearby, Damen proclaimed his joy at this birth, and Gavilan could feel the cat's message ripple down his spine.

His son's downy head searched against his chest for something to suck on, and Gavilan chuckled. Tired and satisfied, he moved to the bed and carefully placed the babe next to his mother's breast so he could nurse without waking her. Pride and wonder at such a miracle washed over him as the dark head sought and found a full breast.

Soft, sucking sounds confirmed his son possessed a strong grasp on things. Gavilan hadn't noticed Laydya's eyes were open, nor her tender smile until he felt her fingers on his cheek as she wiped away the wetness. Searching for something to say, but afraid his throat wouldn't let him, he grinned.

"You lied, woman!"

Both knew what he referred to, and Laydya's answer was almost lost in her throaty laughter.   "I know, but will you still love me forever?"

"Aye, my love . . . you are the prize and forever is the goal!"

THE END

www.ingramcontent.com/pod-product-compliance
Lightning Source LLC
Chambersburg PA
CBHW071244130626
46556CB00003B/1154